THE MACKENZIE REGENT

CAROLINE LEE

ABOUT THIS BOOK

Four years ago, Jaimie Mackenzie lost everything - the woman he loved, the use of his hands, and his honor.

Betrayed by grief and half blinded by drink, Jaimie McKenzie is appalled to discover he has been named his nephew's regent. To cement his position in the clan, he is expected to ally himself with wee Callan's stepmother, a demure painter with a quiet strength, who doesn't flinch from his scars and who seems to have a private purpose on McKenzie land.

Her mission is returning her clan's honor.

Lady Agata is one of the Sinclair Jewels, the eldest daughter of the Laird, intent on solving a decades-old mystery. The only clue she has leads her back to the home of her beloved stepson, Callan. Unfortunately, it includes marriage to a man she's coming to realize isn't as broken as the world thinks...his touch alone is enough to make her yearn for a future with him.

Jaimie can't help returning to the world of the living as his new wife's determination and creativity reawaken his passion. But when his nephew needs them both, can he remember the man he used to be? Agata's newfound family are the only ones who can help her solve the mystery of the missing jewels!

Warning: <u>Scorching hot</u> Highlander romance!

OTHER BOOKS BY CAROLINE LEE

Want the scoop on new books? Join Caroline's Cohort, an exclusive reader group! Or sign up for my mailing list by texting "Caroline" to 42828 to get started!

Hilarious Scottish RomComs:
The Hots for Scots (8 books)
Highlander Ever After (3 books)
Bad in Plaid (6 books)
Second-Chance Manor (2 books)
Those Kilted Bastards (4 books)
Surprise! Dukes (5 books)

Steamy Scottish Historicals:
The Sinclair Jewels (4 books)
The Highland Angels (5 books)

Sensual Historical Westerns:
Black Aces (3 books)
Sunset Valley (3 books)
Everland Ever After (10 books)

The Sweet Cheyenne Quartet (6 books)

Sweet Contemporary Westerns
Quinn Valley Ranch (5 books)
River's End Ranch (14 books)
The Cowboys of Cauldron Valley (7 books)
The Calendar Girls' Ranch (6 books)

Click **here** to find a complete list of Caroline's books.

*Sign up for Caroline's Newsletter to receive exclusive content and freebies, as well as first dibs on her books! Or if newsletters aren't your thing, follow her on **Bookbub** for a quick, concise new release alert every time she publishes a book!*

CHAPTER 1

The Highlands, thirteenth century

"Do ye think we'll ever see her again?"

Agata frowned down at the yellow ochre she was crushing into a fine powder when she answered her sister. "Aye. Dinnae fash, Pearl will find a way home to us."

"But *how?*" Saffy sighed from her spot beside the open window.

Scraping the powder into a small box, Agata hoped their third sister would answer so she could concentrate on her work. The ochre was valuable, and she had no desire to waste any of it because she wasn't paying attention. Carefully, she used the edge of her knife to ensure the last of the powder moved from the bowl to the box, then she let out a breath.

Straightening, she gave her younger sister her attention. "How, what?" she asked, a little peevishly.

Saffy's arms were crossed on the windowsill, her chin propped up on them as she stared toward the mountains, clouded in misty rain. "How are ye so sure Pearl will return?"

Agata stretched her back and worked the kinks out of her neck. "Because she loves the Sinclair people more than anything else in the whole world. She'll find a way back."

"Becoming a nun is a daft idea, even for her," muttered normally good-natured Saffy.

There was a snort from the large bed they'd shared for years. Saffy's twin Citrine was lying there, her feet crossed at the ankles and propped against the wall, her skirts falling well down her legs. Her arms were stacked behind her head as she rolled her eyes at her twin.

"Pearl isnae any closer to becoming a nun than ye or I."

Saffy didn't turn when she jerked her thumb toward Agata, the oldest of them. "Aye, we'd make terrible nuns. But Agata considered it once."

It was true. After David's death and her return to Sinclair lands, Agata had been lost. Ladies in her position had a purpose in life, and marriage to a powerful laird had achieved that for her. But when he'd succumbed to a fever without fathering a child with her, there was no need for her to remain with the Mackenzies, so she'd returned home.

To someone who valued order and control, it was disconcerting to be so unsure of her place in the world. A nunnery would have given her a place, but it wasn't the one she wanted.

"I considered it," she admitted softly. Her gaze dropped to her hands and the smudge of yellow pigment across the pad of her thumb. "But it would be many years afore they'd let me paint."

Although there were monasteries where the nuns produced beautiful religious icons and manuscripts as well as the monks, they didn't allow just anyone to paint. If she had managed to talk Da into sending her, she'd be far from home and years away before being entrusted with a brush again.

And she'd have to give up her dream of being Callan's mother. Even having a place to belong wasn't worth that price.

"Besides," she said, absently rubbing at the stain on her thumb, "Da wouldn't have considered it."

"He did for Pearl," Saffy pointed out needlessly.

That morning, they'd said their tearful goodbyes to their youngest sister. Pearl had objected strongly to the marriage alliance Da had made with Laird Sutherland, and demanded to be allowed to remain home.

Da had denied her.

One thing Pearl had never understood was their position in life. Da was the Sinclair, and as such, he needed to maintain strong alliances. With four daughters—known far and wide as the Sinclair Jewels—marriages were the wisest choices. Their duty demanded they be bartered for their clan's future safety, and Agata had been pleased to fulfill that duty when the Mackenzies had approached Da.

But now… now she wasn't sure where she stood. She was widowed, but her father had already mentioned another marriage agreement. Part of her was desperate with worry about her future, and the other part didn't want to know.

What if her future husband was like David?

On the bed, Citrine snorted dismissively again, and Agata was pleased for the distraction.

"You sound like a hog," she pointed out calmly.

Saffy smothered her laughter as Citrine rolled her eyes.

"Ye're nae lecturing me on my behavior, are ye?"

Agata reached for the small box of yellow pigment and moved it to her shelf of precious paints. "Absolutely not. I wouldnae *think* of pointing out yer numerous deficiencies."

Saffy laughed louder as Citrine pushed herself up on her elbows. As she did so, her skirts dropped further, revealing the knobby knees they all teased her about. Her chin stuck out mulishly as she frowned.

"I might not act like a fancy lady—"

"Or any kind of a lady," Agata hastened to point out.

Citrine huffed and continued, "—But I have more fun."

Agata closed her mouth to keep from smiling, and met her sister's deep, golden gaze. "Aye," she admitted. "Ye do."

Citrine nodded forcefully and said, "Dinnae forget it!" before plopping back down on the bed. In the ensuing silence, Agata stood, wiping down the small desk with a rag, then reaching for her mortar and pestle. She crossed to the ewer of fresh water, moistened the rag, and began to wipe the remains of the yellow powder from the stone.

The sigh from Saffy caught her attention. The twins were younger than Agata and older than Pearl, and although they looked very similar—aside from their eye color—they couldn't be more different. While Citrine was blunt and brooked no nonsense, Saffy was a dreamer. Citrine spent hours each day training with the men, her short stature more than mitigated by her toned muscles from wielding a sword. But Saffy was happier with an old manuscript, her mind full of stories and songs.

Now, she was back to staring out the window, the late spring air misty.

"'Tis terrible traveling weather," she whispered, and Agata knew she was thinking of their youngest sister.

"Pearl will be back," Agata assured her, praying it was true.

From the bed, Citrine hummed in agreement. "O' course she will. 'Tis why Da sent her with the Hound, so he'd be sure of it."

Frowning, Agata turned toward the bed. But it was Saffy—obviously intrigued enough to turn away from the mountain vista—who spoke.

"What do ye mean?"

Lying on her back—her feet still propped on the tapestry on the wall—Citrine managed to shrug. "Ye didn't notice Dougal's irritation? The Sinclair commander should have been the one to escort one of the laird's daughters, aye?"

Agata's lips pulled down. "Ye're right. Why did Da nae send her to the abbey with Dougal, then?"

Citrine smirked and lifted herself up on her elbows once more. "Because…" She raised one brow suggestively. "He kens how Pearl feels about his Hound. Ye havenae seen the way she watches the man?"

"Really?" Saffy gasped, glancing between her two sisters.

Agata feigned nonchalance as she finished wiping down her tools. "Oh, aye, but who *hasnae* looked at the Sinclair Hound that way, hmm?" She carefully placed her mortar and pestle beside her pigments and brushes. "The man is brawny."

"Does he even have a name?" Saffy asked. "The man doesnae speak."

Her twin *tsked*. "Who cares if he doesnae speak? As long as his *tongue* works."

It took a moment for the meaning of her sister's lewd joke to set in, but when it did, Agata did her best to hold in the laughter, not wanting to give Citrine the satisfaction. Saffy wasn't so successful.

"'Tis true! A man who doesnae speak, doesnae make demands, or tell ye what ye can or cannae do!—but still gives ye pleasure…" She sighed dreamily. "'Twould be worth his weight in jewels!"

The image caused Agata to lose her battle. A giggle escaped her, then another, until all three of them were bent over with laughter.

"I want a brawny man who'll give me pleasure!" Saffy pretended to pout, finally curbing her giggles. She ran a hand down the side of her kirtle "If I ask, do ye think Da would arrange such a marriage for me?"

Citrine was still grinning as she swung her bare feet off the bed and leaned forward. "I *think* we'd need to bargain the lost jewels to be assured of *two* such matches for his daughters."

The lost jewels… Something snatched at Agata's memory,

and she wondered what had made her sister think of the missing brooch.

"Besides," Citrine continued, "Da's already made his marriage alliances, even if he willnae tell us who we're to marry. 'Tis the only way to save the clan, at this point."

Her twin nodded, sobering quickly. "I suppose Agata will be next."

"She's been married once, and is the oldest. Da will arrange her marriage quickly."

The four daughters of Duncan Sinclair had been raised in this very room together. Aside from the months Agata spent as Lady Mackenzie, the girls passed their evenings gossiping and giggling about men, dreams, and irritations. Over the years, they'd turned to their eldest sister for advice and guidance, and Agata had been pleased to lead them wisely. Even in the matter of marriage, she was the most experienced, and had answered their questions about the bedding act in as much detail as they wanted.

But they also knew how close the Sinclair clan was to catastrophe. With only daughters, they'd often discussed who would follow their father as laird. That's why their marriages were so vital to the clan's future.

That's why she prayed bold Citrine was correct, and Agata would be the one married first. She *was* the oldest Sinclair Jewel, and needed to find her place. She'd been surprised when Da had told her he'd made a match for her less than a sennight ago. As with the twins, he hadn't yet named her groom, but Agata hadn't stopped wondering what kind of man chose her, when her younger sisters were still—*mostly*—pure?

Was he a laird? Or had Da given her to someone else? A warrior? A merchant?

A man like David?

"'Tis unsettling to think of being sold," Saffy said quietly from her window seat.

Agata forced a smile. "Dinnae worry. Marriage will bring ye purpose and a place." *Order. A proper future.* "And passion. And bairns." Unconsciously, her hand fell to cover her womb, but she turned the gesture at the last moment and smoothed her gown over her stomach. "'Tis good to be married."

Citrine didn't even look at her when she muttered, "Ye're no' good at lying."

Her twin's clear blue eyes were sad when she nodded to Agata. "Do ye miss wee Callan terribly, Agata?"

Callan.

In the half a year since she'd been widowed, Agata had done an admirable job of returning to her old life, pretending that her time with the Mackenzies was a distant dream. But sometimes at night, she'd remember the feel of small arms around her neck, or sticky kisses on her cheek, or dirty hand-prints on her gown, and she'd *ache* to hold the boy again.

She swallowed, knowing her smile had turned brittle. "I ken he's happy and well cared for, and that's what matters. His uncle will…" The words caught in her throat. Truthfully, she knew nothing about David's younger brother, only that her husband had thought him a disappointing wastrel.

Callan was only seven years old, and as David's son, was destined to be the next laird. But he had many years before he'd be able to rule. Agata knew David's aunt would ensure the boy was safe and happy, and with Callan's uncle acting as regent until the lad came of age, everything would be fine with the Mackenzies.

So why did her heart ache to think of Callan growing up without her?

Saffy's eyes were full of pity and her smile was false when she nodded. "Oh, aye. The wee lad will be fine. And soon ye'll have the chance to be a mother again." She shot her twin a glare. "Right, Citrine? Da will make good matches for his Jewels?"

But rather than reassure her, Citrine frowned down at the rushes. "Oh, aye," she mimicked. "Naught but the best for the Sinclair Jewels."

The jewels... why were they thinking of them? Agata frowned in thought, her gaze darting around their chamber. What had made her remember?

She gasped out loud as her attention fell on a bundle of material atop Pearl's chest.

Her sisters watched as Agata hurried across the chamber, reaching for the things Pearl had left with them yesterday evening. Their youngest sister was always helping someone in the village or visiting clan members. She made a point of bringing food and companionship to those who were some-times forgotten, including Elspeth, their old nurse. Yesterday, Pearl had visited the woman's cottage, then returned for the evening meal before going to Da's solar to deliver her ultimatum.

But before she'd gone, she'd given Agata this bundle from Elspeth. At the time, Agata had only glanced at it, too distraught at the thought of Pearl leaving to really notice it, but now...

"Ah!" she declared triumphantly as she held aloft the old tapestry. "The jewels!"

Saffy was beside her in a moment. "No..." she breathed softly, reaching for the image. "I dinnae believe it."

Her fingers hovered above the threads, and Agata saw them tremble slightly.

"Impossible," Citrine stated definitively. "The jewels have been missing for generations."

"And this tapestry looks at least that old," Saffy whispered reverently.

While Agata knew paints, Saffy was the scholar of the sisters, and if she said these threads were that old, Agata would believe her. Gently, she draped the small tapestry across her forearm, and crossed to the bed. Citrine stepped out of the way, but when Agata placed the piece of material down, she felt her sisters peering over her shoulders.

"Beautiful," Saffy breathed.

It *was*. The tapestry was no larger than one of Agata's paintings, but full of color. The clan name had been woven in blues and greens across the top, and in the center…

In the center was a bright green circle containing four smaller circles, arranged at the cardinal points. Decorative scrollwork was picked out in dark threads, delineating each sphere. The circle at the top was brown, intricately stitched to show shades ranging from sable to topaz. The circle to the right was a bright blue, the same color as the "S" in "Sinclair," while the bottom one was a yellow dark enough to be called gold. The fourth circle was a beautiful white, which seemed to shimmer gray, despite the age of the threads.

Agata exhaled softly. She'd glimpsed the image when Pearl had handed it to her, but had been too distracted to realize what it meant. "The jewels," she whispered.

Generations ago, the pride of the Sinclair treasury had gone missing. Elspeth had always told them the Sinclair line would end if the jewels remained lost, and only the bravest and worthiest of the Sinclair warriors would be able to restore the jewels and the clan's power.

Most of them had thought it a myth, but their mother hadn't.

Citrine leaned around Agata and pointed to each of the circles in turn, careful not to actually touch the ancient tapestry. "Agate. Sapphire. Citrine. Pearl," she finished grimly. Then she stabbed one finger toward the outer circle. "And malachite?"

The stones were all from the highlands. When each of her daughters had been born, their mother had named them for the colors of their eyes. Agata's eyes were a dark brown with gold flecks. Saffy's were a bright blue, Citrine a pale brown, and Pearl, a blue so light it seemed gray.

The sisters had always known they were named for Highland jewels, and it was where the silly tradition of calling them the Sinclair Jewels had begun. But knowing they were named for the jewels in the missing Sinclair brooch, and *seeing* the brooch, were entirely different matters.

"Is that… us?" Saffy whispered.

Citrine made a noise somewhere between disgust and disbelief, and spun away. Agata's hand found Saffy's as they watched their sister stomp across the chamber and back, her bare feet slapping against the stone and rushes.

"If Mother named us after some stones in an old brooch, did that mean she'd seen the jewels?" Citrine demanded, clearly not expecting an answer. "Or had she just seen this daft —" She waved her hand irritably toward the tapestry on the bed, her jaw working as she tried to find the right word. Finally, she ended with an angry, "*Bah!*"

"Da would ken," Saffy offered hesitantly.

But Agata sniffed. "The man willnae tell us who we are to marry. He's good at secrets."

"Aye!" Citrine whirled with her hands on her hips and a frown on her lips. "But that willnae stop us from asking him. *And* Elspeth."

"Mayhap the tapestry can tell us more." Saffy pulled away and leaned over the weaving.

"Like what?" snapped her twin.

"Like what happened to the jewels."

Agata felt her heart begin to pound at Saffy's distracted statement. *Find the missing jewels? Was that possible?* The sisters had spoken of them for years; she remembered evenings spent lying in bed well after dark, whispering theories back and forth. Saffy's suggestions were always romantic and unrealistic, while Citrine's guesses had involved pirates and bandits.

But Agata had never even been sure the jewels had existed.

She leaned over Saffy's shoulder, examining the delicate tapestry. Although their mother had died soon after Pearl's birth, Elspeth had known the woman—and their grandmother—well. Their old nurse had raised them with stories of the famed brooch, much larger than a man's fist and fashioned from malachite and gold. Had it been real? Was it hidden somewhere with the jewels still intact?

Would it be possible to find it again?

"The clan doesnae need saving!"

Agata glanced over her shoulder at Citrine, who was glaring at them both, as if daring them to contradict her.

"What do ye mean?"

"The legend!" Citrine scowled at the tapestry. "Elspeth told us the Sinclairs would fall without the jewels, aye? But we're—"

"Da has only daughters," Saffy murmured distractedly, her hands braced on the coverlet on either side of the tapestry, her nose only inches from the threads. "If he doesnae remarry and sire a son, his line will end."

Agata's eyes widened as she met Citrine's, whose anger slowly turned to shock. Aye, they'd known the clan was in danger—hence the importance of their marriage alliances. But could their current state be the fate the legend foretold? Was the Sinclair name bound to fall because Da had no son to become laird after him?

"Bollocks!" Citrine slammed one fist into the opposite palm with enough force to make Agata jump. "That'll no' happen!"

Agata crossed her arms and raised her brows in silent question.

"I'll no' let the Sinclairs fall. Remember what Elspeth told us?" Citrine glared in defiance. "If the jewels are lost forever, our line is doomed."

"A moment ago, ye said it was nonsense," Agata pointed out.

"*'Tis nonsense,* but I'll no' let it happen," Citrine repeated angrily, if illogically. "We'll find the damn brooch and ensure the Sinclair name is—"

Unimpressed by her twin's ranting, Saffy straightened away from the tapestry. "How?"

Citrine scowled. "How what?"

"How will we find the jewels? They've been missing for years, and this cannae be solved by swinging a sword at it."

Her twin's scowl didn't ease as she leveled a long finger at Saffy. "Verra few things cannae be solved by swinging a sword at them."

Saffy scoffed, likely already composing a long treatise in her mind on the history of the jewels. "Surely *someone* should ken the secret. We'll just ask—"

"Nay!" Citrine's denial was forceful enough to make her sisters startle. She frowned fiercely while pinning them with a serious glare. "This is *our* business. If we are to find the jewels, we *cannae* be spreading our information around." When Agata opened her mouth, Citrine cut her off. "I mean it! This *must* be kept a secret, if we're to succeed."

Agata's brows rose. It sounded as if this daring sister of hers was serious about hunting down the lost jewels. And to her surprise, Saffy was nodding.

"I hate to say it, but Citrine is correct. If we hope to find them and save the clan, we must keep our hunt a secret."

"Swear it," Citrine demanded.

"I swear," her twin answered immediately.

Both turned to Agata, who actually took a step back under their combined gazes. They were serious! They were planning on hunting down the jewels and serious about keeping it a secret?

"Agata?" the twins prompted in unison, not a little eerily.

She blew out a disbelieving breath. "Aye! All right, aye, I swear I'll keep the hunt a secret."

"Ye'll not share our reasons for asking so many questions?" Citrine asked.

"Da might—"

Saffy was shaking her head. "If we told him *why* we were hunting, he'd tell us we're foolish. We can ask for help, though, aye?" she asked her twin.

Citrine nodded. "Aye, we'll take help where we can, but no one must ken why."

Agata threw up her hands. "Fine, I swear. Ye two are ridiculous."

Saffy frowned. "'Twas Citrine's idea."

"*Ye* agreed!" Citrine pointed a finger at her twin's chest. "And for that matter, what was that '*I hate to say it, but Citrine is correct*' nonsense?"

Used to her sisters' bickering, Agata pushed them from her mind and stepped up beside the tapestry again. While the twins argued behind her, she peered at the weaving. The circles within the circle *had* to represent the jewels set in the brooch. If they were as large as the legend said, the jewels must be quite valuable. Is that why the whole thing had gone missing? The stones were native, but still worth more than the gold they were set in, if they really were flawless. But the scrollwork of the brooch itself appeared intricate…

Frowning, Agata peered closer. In fact, the ornate decoration around the jewels almost looked like words.

Behind her, Citrine had just launched into one of her favorite lectures about strength and determination, but Agata strained her eyes to make sense of the jumble of squiggles she was seeing.

"Mackenzie," she whispered.

Was that really what it said, or just a name she wanted to see? Thinking about Callan might've made the clan's name appear at the front of her mind, but it was difficult to argue with the collection of letters before her. "Mackenzie," she said again.

"What?" Saffy questioned as the twins moved up on either side.

Agata took a breath and pointed at the intricate design around the edge of the brooch. "Is it my imagination, or does that say 'Mackenzie'?"

Citrine leaned closer, then snapped straight once more with a curse she'd learned from the warriors. "Why would *our* brooch say Mackenzie?"

Her sister had apparently gone from doubting the veracity of the tapestry to claiming ownership of the once-mythical jewels. Agata shrugged. "Maybe the Mackenzies have it?"

"Ye were there for nigh a year, Agata," Saffy pointed out. "Did ye see any of the jewels or hear any rumors indicating they'd stolen them?"

Stolen? Agata shook her head. "As far as I ken, my marriage to David was the first connection between the Sinclairs and Mackenzies in many years."

"So, they *must* have stolen them!" Citrine slammed her fist into her palm again. "Come on, we'll ask Da about this."

She stormed, still barefoot, out of the room. Hurrying to keep up, Agata watched Saffy lean back over the tapestry, apparently not as interested in what Da had to say. But Agata… she knew their father wouldn't tell what he knew. The man still hadn't told her who she was to marry, only to make herself ready soon. Why would he tell them what he knew about the tapestry or the missing jewels… or the Mackenzies?

With the Hound away from the holding, escorting Pearl to the Abbey, there was no one standing guard outside Da's solar. Citrine pushed open the heavy door, and Agata wasn't sure if she was disappointed or relieved their father wasn't there. The room was empty, with weak afternoon light filtering through the window.

Citrine immediately crossed to the row of shelves which held many scrolls, muttering to herself as she pulled out random ones. Agata, unsure what they were looking for, crossed to Da's desk. It was cluttered with parchments; letters, contracts, and petitions all seemed to merge into one pile, but her name caught her eye.

She nudged a letter out of the way and pulled out an official parchment. A marriage contract… with *her* name on it.

Her heart began to pound as she read the words.

Whereas… alliance… familiarity… acceptable…

She was betrothed. To… her eyes dropped to the bottom, to the Mackenzie seal. She was betrothed to Jaimie Mackenzie, David's wastrel younger brother.

The parchment fluttered to the desk, and Agata caught the corner to keep herself upright. She was betrothed to Jaimie? She was going back to the Mackenzie holding?

She'd be able to hold Callan again.

"Agata?" Citrine called out, staring at her. "Ye look all pale. Come help me."

"I'm…" Agata took a breath. "I'll be fine."

Her sister didn't seem to notice. "Good. Then get over here and help me find some kind of proof against the Mackenzies. We need them to look for our jewels!"

"I'll do it," Agata whispered.

"What?"

"I'll do it," she repeated, stronger. Her gaze dropped to the marriage contract on the desk in front of her, and she pressed her fingertips to the space between her name and Jaimie's. "I'll look for the jewels."

"When?" Citrine demanded.

"After my wedding."

CHAPTER 2

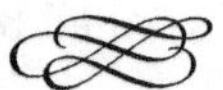

Jaimie Mackenzie was drunk.

He couldn't remember a time he *wasn't*, at least a little. Of course, he couldn't remember much of anything, being drunk.

That was the point.

In the months since he'd been back home, he'd turned David's solar into *his*. By that, of course, he meant he'd tossed as many pieces of parchment into the fire as Edward, the seneschal, would allow. David had always been so serious about clan business, so determined to do things the "right" way… and Jaimie wasn't David. Not even a little.

So, the damn contracts and letters and whatever else a laird needed to know about was left for Edward. He knew anything he left lying on David's wide desk was as likely to wind up burnt as read.

And Jaimie used the space for drinking.

This afternoon he sat in David's chair, his booted feet propped up on the desk, a flagon of ale dangling from his ruined fingers. Through lank hair, he glared at the one thing on the desk he hadn't burned in all these months; he'd never been *that* drunk.

The map had been carved before his grandfather's time and was a thing of beauty. Even with the paint all-but-chipped away, it was clear the colors had been bright and bold. Some long-ago artist—someone with ten whole fingers, damn him—had outlined the Highlands and Lowlands, and surrounded them with fanciful representations of sea monsters and ships. The clan boundaries had been carved as well, or at least where the boundaries had been all those years ago. Even without color, the wood was smooth and perfect and calming.

Remembering long ago evenings spent pouring over the map with David and their father, Jaimie winced and lifted the flagon to his lips. He and David both had learned geography from that map.

They'd learned how to be hard from their father.

The ale was nearly gone. How much effort would it take to get more? Edward had probably sent up a half-full ewer anyhow. The old man—along with Aunt Jean—was always harping on him to drink less. Still, if Jaimie dragged his sorry arse to the door and started hollering, surely *someone* would bring him more, aye? He was the laird's regent, after all.

As if conjured, steps in the corridor outside told him someone approached. Through a muddled mind, Jaimie strained to listen. Was it the distinctive shuffle of that young serving wench—what was her name? Morag? Or one of his brother's warriors sent with another nagging task and possibly more ale as well?

"Jaimie Mackenzie!" came the feminine call from outside the door. "Ye'd better be decent this time."

Damn. It was his aunt, which meant there'd be no more ale.

When Aunt Jean pushed her way into the solar, Jaimie brightened momentarily to see Edward behind her. But the old man's arms were empty of another ewer of ale, so Jaimie slouched, dejected in David's chair once more.

"Hello, Aunt," he drawled, allowing his head to fall back

against the hard wood of the tall chair. "Come to spy on me again?"

The short, stout woman just scowled and brushed away his comment with an irritated wave. The last time she'd entered the solar without knocking or calling, he'd been in the middle of some… *business*. The wench from the brothel in the village had been bent over the desk, facing the door, when Jean had entered.

Jaimie always took them from behind so they wouldn't have to look him in the face. Because he was a kind man.

Still, that hadn't helped the poor lass's embarrassment as she'd squealed at the interruption, pulled down her skirts, and fled, pushing by the exasperated, older woman.

Aunt Jean had made a point of calling out since then.

"Drunk again, are ye, lad? In the middle of the day?"

He set the flagon on the desk beside him. "Not drunk enough, I'm beginning to suspect. What do ye want?"

The short dragon moved to the window, tugging it open, and allowing the sunlight and damnable fresh air to sweep through the room. Jaimie winced and shut his eyes to the affront, knowing his aunt had intended to punish him for his lack of manners.

"I *want* what I've wanted for half a year now, lad." She turned to face him, so the early summer sunshine outlined her outdated wimple and made her glow like some kind of nagging saint. "I *want* ye to quit feeling sorry for yerself, get off yer arse, and be the man wee Callan needs ye to be."

Wee Callan.

Jaimie ignored the way his stomach clenched at the boy's name. He'd come back home months ago, after Aunt Jean's letter had reached him about David's illness, and had seen Callan for the first time since Aileen's death.

The experience had sent him lunging for a flagon of ale.

"He doesnae need *me*," Jaimie snarled, his ruined fingers

tightening around the flagon. "He has ye two. He has the entire clan."

"He needs his *uncle*." Jean stepped toward the desk, her lips tight. "He needs his *laird*."

This time, Jaimie growled, "I'm no laird."

"Ye're all but!" His aunt threw up her hands. "'Tis yer duty to protect no' just him, but all of us. 'Tis yer duty to protect the Mackenzies, Jaimie."

"Ye can take that *duty* and shove it up—"

"Milord," Edward interrupted, stepping forward to draw Jaimie's attention. "'Tis done."

Irritated at having his rant cut off, Jaimie blinked at the older man. "*What's* done?"

"The alliance, milord."

The way he said "alliance," ominous and foreboding, sent the hairs on Jaimie's forearms standing up. Without meaning to, his gaze dropped to the desk, then flicked to the empty shelves along the wall. What alliance? Had he missed burning something? Had the damned seneschal gone behind his back?

Before he could ask, Aunt Jean *tsked* loudly. "Whether or no' ye want the duty, Jaimie, it falls on ye to protect the clan. The easiest way is through a strong alliance."

She held out her hand, palm up, and Edward hurried forward to lay a scroll in her palm. Where had he been holding that? Jaimie shook his head once in a hopeless attempt to clear his vision and mind.

"Now, yer brother kenned how important it was to keep the powerful Sutherlands from our borders." Jean unrolled the parchment as she spoke. "'Tis why he married one of the Sinclair Jewels. With his death, the marriage—and thus the alliance—was voided, which could mean disaster if the Sutherlands are ever bright enough to ally with the Rosses or MacKays."

Jaimie did his best to follow her brisk speech, but his head felt too heavy. With the sunlight and the fresh air swirling around him, he wondered how rude it would be to demand his aunt take the crusty old seneschal and leave him to die in peace.

"What are ye saying, Aunt?" he all but sighed, willing her to get to the point quickly.

With a flourish, she spread the parchment on the desk beside the map, nudging his boots off the wood as she did so. As his feet hit the floor, Jaimie was propelled upright with a curse.

A curse he repeated when he shut one eye and tried to read the letters which swam on the contract.

Whereas... alliance... familiarity... acceptable...

"Jean?" he croaked in dread.

"'Tis a marriage contract, lad," she said, not unkindly. "The Sinclair has agreed to send us one of his daughters again. Ye'll be wed as soon as she arrives."

Jaimie's dark gaze snapped back up to his aunt's, but the little dragon had the nerve to smile and nod in encouragement. She wasn't the only one; Edward was bouncing with excitement.

"And ye'll never guess, milord!"

Shaking his head in denial, Jaimie changed his mind and agreed with the old man. "Ye're right, Edward. I'd never guess."

"'Tis *her*, laird! The Sinclair is sending *her* back!"

God, this was making less and less sense. A marriage? Him? His aunt's purpose sounded reasonable, although Jaimie could barely understand. If he'd been sober—if he'd been a better man—he might have been able to admit she was right. But *married*? Yoked to one woman for the rest of his life? Another spoiled, cruel, power-hungry noblewoman?

He shuddered. *Nay.* Nay, he wouldn't be able to stand another woman like Aileen in his life.

But the seneschal's excitement had penetrated his dull thoughts. "Her?" he mumbled.

"Lady Agata, milord!" Edward declared joyfully. "Yer brother's wife. She's much loved here, and although 'tis unorthodox to send her here to be yer bride, we're all pleased."

Blearily, Jaimie turned his disbelieving gaze to his aunt. But the old woman's smile grew as she nodded, confirming the seneschal's words.

"Agata is a dear woman, Jaimie, and I was thrilled when Duncan Sinclair suggested her. She kens the keep, and is strong enough to impose some order and control here again. Besides, she's already been the object of an alliance between our clans once afore. It made sense for her to return."

"My brother's wife?" Jaimie rasped.

"Aye. Ye never met her, of course, what with ye being so *needed* at court, and then at yer cousin's holding. That's the excuse ye gave us for being away so long, aye? But being away, ye never met Agata. She's dear to all of us, especially Callan. She'll be a welcome lady of the keep once more."

Jaimie's dull gaze landed on the map again. Spread out before him was the might of the Sutherlands, their power sitting squarely in the middle of the Highlands to the south of the Sinclairs. He blinked, the lines on the map wavering before his eyes. *Married?* They wanted him to marry? Marry to protect the clan, marry to ensure a powerful alliance to keep the Sutherlands at bay.

But what kind of man married his brother's widow? What kind of man married a woman who'd never look him in the eyes, never think of him with anything beyond pity?

And what kind of man sent his daughter to marry someone like *him*?

"Come now, lad," Jean said softly, moving to stand on his left side.

Jaimie didn't hide his wince when he felt her hand drop to his shoulder comfortingly, but doubted she saw it past his curtain of lank, dark hair. Besides, the damage to the left side of his face meant few noticed any movement there at all.

Whether she saw his reaction or not, his aunt continued in a soothing tone. "We ken marriage wasnae yer plan, but yer plan needs to change for the good of the clan. I acted as Callan's representative in the negotiations with Sinclair, but ye are his regent. None of us can force ye to marry."

Marry.

Could he do it? Could he shackle himself to one woman? Slowly, still staring at the map, he shook his head. It wasn't worth it. Not for himself, but for *her.*

"*Jaimie,*" his aunt cajoled. "The days of yer youth are past. Ye might be a charmer and a lover, but—"

He cut her off with a snarl, snatching the flagon off the table and downing the remainder of the ale, not even caring when the vicious movement caused the amber liquid to splash and dribble through his sparse, ill-kept beard and onto his shirt. His throat worked frantically as he guzzled the liquid, as if he could erase her words.

Charmer? Lover?

Not since winter had robbed him of his looks, his hands. Not since Aileen.

The ale was gone too soon, but his heart was still tight from anger. With a snarl, he hurled the empty flagon at the window. With the room spinning the way it was, he missed entirely, but the sudden explosion of liquid as it sprayed over the stone, caused Edward to step backward with a yelp.

"Jaimie."

He might've ignored his aunt's soft call had she not placed her palm on his chin and turned his face toward hers. Suddenly feeling too weak to resist, he just scowled at the old dragon. He'd had enough pity, the awkwardness as people tried not to stare at his scars.

But when Aunt Jean wanted something, she was a force to be reckoned with.

"Lad, ye're doing the right thing, and ye ken it. After all," she flashed a quick, almost sad smile, "Ye're too old to be waiting on yer south-land treasure."

At her version of the old proverb, Jaimie pulled his chin from her grasp, not sure if he was defeated yet.

Yer treasure land is to the south. Yer treasure lies in the south-lands. Waiting on yer south-land treasure.

They were all versions of the same theme, and Jaimie had grown up knowing the elders who used it all meant the same thing. He was always looking *elsewhere* for fulfillment. It was why, well before Father had passed on and David took up the mantle of lairdship, Jaimie had made a place for himself at court. He'd spent so many years as an emissary, traveling between holdings and castles and courts, enjoying the exciting differences and treasures to be found.

Aye, his treasure had always been someplace else, not here on Mackenzie lands.

But now he was stuck here, for Callan's sake. And because fate had damaged him beyond use.

Could he be useful again? If only by marrying the Sinclair lass? His brother's widow?

"Lady Jean? Lady Jean!"

All thoughts of marriage fled with the sound of small steps in the corridor. Aunt Jean's face bloomed into a genuine smile. Just before the steps reached the door, they halted, as if a running little boy had halted to adjust his breathing and practice decorum, the way his father had instructed him.

When Callan finally stepped through the open door, a proud smile on his face and a piece of parchment clutched in front of him, Jaimie's heart lurched. He squeezed his eyes shut so he wouldn't have to see the boy's confusion and embarrassment at accidentally stumbling upon his crippled uncle.

But he still heard it.

"Oh! I…" A shuffle, as if the boy debated backing out again. "I was looking for ye, Lady Jean," he finished quietly.

Lady Jean. She'd been David's aunt, the same as she was Jaimie's, their father's sister who'd never married. Growing up, she'd been their dragon, as strong and sure as Father had been, but full of compassion as well. She'd been the one to encourage them, to push them to be better men.

And still, David had called her *lady* instead of *aunt*, and raised his son the same.

Jean's gasp was proud. "Oh, Callan, another masterpiece?"

Curious, Jaimie opened his right eye so there was only one set of dragon and boy and seneschal floating around the room. Jean stood beside Callan, peering over his shoulder and making interested cooing sounds as he pointed out various things on the parchment in front of him.

Jaimie dropped his hands to the chair arms, forcing himself upright in an effort to see what they were doing. The movement caught his aunt's attention, and she looked up with a smile.

"Wee Callan has become quite the artist, Jaimie. Would ye care to see this beauty?"

I care naught for beauty.

He wanted to yell the words, to tell them all to leave him to his peace, to ignore the revelations of the last moments. He wanted to hurt them the way he hurt.

But staring blearily at the hopeful look on the boy's face, so like Aileen, Jaimie knew he wouldn't.

"Aye," he managed to croak.

It was impossible to miss the way the boy didn't move until Jean nudged him, pushing him toward the large desk. But eventually, he was standing to Jaimie's left, where his aunt had been.

His ruined side.

What remained of Jaimie's fingers tightened around the arms of the chair. With the boy standing so close, he itched to reach out. To touch him.

For so many years, he'd relied on touch. It was what he was known for, Jaimie Mackenzie was a charmer, a lover. But in the last years, so few touched him.

And the boy? Callan would surely flinch if Jaimie tried now.

"What is it?" he asked gruffly, knowing he sounded like a bear.

"I… I drew this."

Callan placed the parchment on the desk atop the wooden map. It was covered in charcoal, a simple line drawing, smudged here and there. Jaimie leaned forward, attempting to make sense of it.

When he did, he sucked in a breath.

It might've been simple, but it was a fairly decent representation of a valley with the loch shining below. What he'd thought were random smudges now seemed carefully placed, to indicate distant snowfields on the north side of the mountain or the field of wheat in the meadow below.

Jaimie closed one eye again, hoping to bring the scene into better focus. The lad had even added a few faint lines which looked like the sun's reflection on the water. How had he managed that with only charcoal? And at age seven?

The itching was back in his palms. He wanted to hug the boy, to tell him he was proud. But instead, Jaimie forced himself to lean back once more.

"'Tis good," he said. "Ye have a gift."

"Oh, no," Callan was quick to deny it as he snatched up the parchment, but Jaimie saw the way the boy's cheeks turned pink as his lips pulled up. Because of a compliment? "Lady Agata taught me p—per—perspective."

Jean smiled proudly at the boy, but Jaimie didn't know if it was because of his manners or his use of the word. Jaimie's tongue flicked out over his dry lower lip, suddenly ravenous for a drink.

"Lady Agata?"

The boy nodded eagerly, holding the parchment in front of him like a shield. "My father's wife. She was verra nice."

Nice. Orderly. Well-loved.

She sounded like someone who didn't deserve to be married to a failure of a man.

Jean must've seen something in his expression, because she clasped Callan's shoulder and drew his attention. "Yer uncle is impressed, lad. Will ye save this piece or scrape it as Agata taught ye?"

To Jaimie's surprise, the boy seemed to seriously consider it. Were other seven-year-olds so intense? He remembered little of being that age, except endless energy and optimism.

"I'm no' verra good at it," Callan finally confessed with a shrug. "Do ye think I might keep it as it is?"

Jean nodded. "If yer nurse will allow it, I willnae object. And neither will yer uncle."

They both turned to Jaimie, who reeled back under the combined weight of their identical-blue Mackenzie gazes. Jean's expression was commanding, Callan's hopeful.

Hopeful? Hopeful Jaimie wouldn't deny him the chance to keep his own artwork?

Then he remembered David, who saw most art as frivolous. Useless. Callan had learned from his father's wife when David had still been alive. Had they both been subjected to David's hard views on the subject?

Jaimie's head began to pound, trying not to remember the way home had been when David ruled here. When

Aileen had been alive. When Father's way had been the "right" way.

"Aye," he mumbled, dropping his forehead into his palm, resisting the urge to squeeze his temples. "I mean, nay. The drawing is yers, and—and perfect. Keep it."

Something passed between the other two, because Callan's, "Thank ye, milord," was hesitant. But Jaimie didn't look up, not even when Jean escorted the boy to the door and bid him to wash for supper.

The silence stretched. He didn't even hear her footsteps and began to hope she'd left as well. Left him to silence and his drinking. Was there more ale? He couldn't recall. Had he demanded more or only thought of it? Was it possible to fall asleep upright, his head in his hand? Or would his elbow slip from the arm of the chair…?

"Jaimie."

At his aunt's gentle call, he jerked upright, slamming the back of his head into the wood of the chair. He slid down with a moan, half in pain and half in disappointment that she was still there, even if Edward had apparently left with Callan.

There was a smile in her voice when she nagged him again. "He's a good lad, and ye handled that well."

He didn't want or need her compliments, and made sure his scowl said so.

Under her wimple, one dark brow raised in challenge. "Ye've been home for months, Jaimie, and done everything in yer power to avoid the wee lad. But he's yer responsibility, the same as the clan. Ye need to protect him, to raise him to be the man—"

He slammed his palms down on either side of the wooden map and leaned forward. "To be the man his father was? The man his grandfather was?" he interrupted her. "Hard and unbending?" *Cruel? Cold?* But he didn't say that—Father had been her brother, after all.

Jean's expression softened. "I was going to say, *to be the man ye are.*"

He wished he had another flagon. He'd drain it and toss it at *her* this time. Instead, he satisfied himself with scowling, his head pounding from the drink and the sunlight and the blow from the chair and the feats of concentration he'd had to perform.

"I'm no' the man he needs to be."

"Ye used to be, Jaimie."

The pity in her voice sent him over the edge. With a snarl, he propelled himself to his feet, holding to the edge of the desk to keep himself upright. "What do ye want, ye dragon? Why are ye still here, tormenting me? Do ye hate me so?"

But she just clucked her tongue and drew herself up, managing to look somehow taller than she was. She twitched one eyebrow again in challenge. "I *torment* ye, lad, because I expect better from ye. I expect ye to do yer duty by the lad, to teach and protect—"

"Fine!" he nearly roared. "I'll do yer precious duty!"

"No' mine," she snapped, "but yers. 'Tis *yer* duty to ensure our alliance with the Sinclairs is strong! Yers to marry the lass and—"

"Aye! *Aye!*" he repeated at the top of his lungs. Then, his strength drained by anger and sorrow and ale—always far too much ale—he slid back into David's hated chair. "Aye," he whispered on a wince. "I'll marry the lass."

Jean pounced on the agreement. "Ye will?"

"Will ye leave me to die in peace if I repeat myself?"

She waved away his dramatic words. "And once she's here, ye'll treat her well?"

There'd been a note of... of *something* in her question. Jaimie met his aunt's gaze, and was surprised to see real concern there. She was afraid he'd... what? Hurt the lass? Treat her coldly?

It wasn't up to *him*. He was certain once Lady Agata returned to the Mackenzie keep, she'd realize what a horrible mistake she'd made.

Staring into his aunt's blue eyes, Jaimie forced himself to rasp out, "She'll hate ye for it, ye ken."

"For arranging this marriage?" His aunt didn't wait for his agreement, before she shook her head briskly. "She will no' hate me."

"She will," he repeated. "Ye've done her a grave disservice." He flexed his ruined fingers.

"Because ye're no longer handsome?" Jean scoffed. "Ye have a low opinion of her already, I see."

How could he not? She'd been married to David. Surely, for all his aunt's praise, Lady Agata was as spoiled and flighty as Aileen.

But regardless of his appearance, that wasn't why his soon-to-be-wife would abhor him. He'd lost his honor long ago, and no woman deserved to be yoked to a man like him.

Before he could possibly find words to explain, his aunt clucked her tongue again and turned toward the door, her gown billowing around her.

"She'll no' hate me *or ye*, Jaimie. Afore the year is out, she'll thank me for arranging this marriage." With one hand on the door, she threw a smirk over her shoulder. "And so will ye."

Long after she left, long after he heard the noise of supper preparations filtering up from the great hall, Jaimie sat and stared at the damn map. The Sinclair holding stood at the northern tip of the Highlands, and an alliance with them was smart indeed. David had probably made the contract fully aware of what it meant.

But Jaimie had spent years making much more informal alliances for much more informal reasons. *Touch. Pleasure. Passion.* He'd always assumed if he'd marry, it would be for one —or all—of those.

He'd been foolish enough to believe in love. But he'd been a different man then, a man who deserved love. A *whole* man. Now, the best he could manage was marrying for duty. But he wouldn't be *pleased* about it.

And no matter what Aunt Jean said, he knew Lady Agata wouldn't either.

CHAPTER 3

THE SAME CHAPEL. The same priest. The difference was that
for this wedding, no one was in attendance.

Agata tightened her grip on the little bouquet of rosemary
to hide her shaking hands and did her best to stop comparing
her two weddings. It had been early last year when she'd stood
in this small chapel within the walls of the Mackenzie keep,
and pledged herself to David, the Mackenzie. He'd been strong
and stoic, and Agata had soon realized it was no act; she and
her new husband were ill-suited.

"'Twill be fine, lass."

The whispered comfort came from Lady Jean Mackenzie,
her husband's aunt. Or her soon-to-be-husband's aunt. Sweet
Mother Mary, but it would be hard not to compare Jaimie to
his older brother. She'd been near frantic over the thought
since discovering her fate in the form of the contract in Da's
solar. But no matter how nervous she was, she hadn't objected
to the match for three very good reasons:

One: She'd been raised as a lady, and knew her purpose in
life was to make alliances and have bairns. She could do
neither sitting at home, taking no chances.

Two: The marriage contract was a convenient way to return to the Mackenzies, which would allow her time and opportunity to hunt for either the Sinclair jewels, or more clues to their whereabouts. Whoever made that tapestry—and Elspeth had been unable to help them, only knowing Da's mother had passed it to her before the older woman's death—had seen fit to include the Mackenzie name in it. Therefore, a clue—or the jewels themselves!—must be found here at the Mackenzie holding.

And three: Callan. In the months since she'd said her good-byes to her husband's son, she'd felt as if her heart wasn't whole. Although they'd had less than a year together when she'd been married to David, she thought of Callan as her own. Leaving him so soon after his father's death had been cruel.

So Agata took a deep breath, forced a tight smile, and nodded to Jean. "Aye," she whispered. "I ken."

Everything *would* be fine. No matter if her new husband was like his brother. She'd survived marriage to David, and she'd survive marriage to Jaimie. And in doing so, she'd have an opportunity to help save her clan, and she'd be with Callan. What more could she want?

Swallowing, she tamped down the traitorous little voice which whispered *"love"* in the back of her mind. Callan loved her, and that would be enough.

When Jean smiled, the old woman's face was transformed. She'd been such a comfort during Agata's first stay with the Mackenzies and had welcomed the younger woman back with open arms. Although she'd never married, Jean was as loving as any mother. And during Agata's first marriage, Jean had been the one to care for her and answer her questions about her husband's family.

"Ye'll find yer south-land treasure, I ken it."

The old saying was one she hadn't heard since returning

home. In fact, she'd *only* heard it here on Mackenzie lands, from Jean and David and a few others, and it seemed to mean something different to each person. To Jean, it was always an encouragement and meant the dear lady truly wanted the best for Agata.

So Agata smiled in return, a real smile. She forced herself to forget her fears and focus on the benefits of this marriage, and made sure that excitement showed through.

When Jean placed a hand on her forearm, Agata wasn't sure if she'd succeeded or not.

"Jaimie isnae like his brother, Agata," Jean whispered.

She'd said that before, but was it a good thing or a bad thing?

Agata nodded and turned her attention to the priest once more. "Aye, 'tis obvious. For one thing, David was always prompt."

She'd arrived that morning with her escort, and even now, Da's commander Dougal scowled as he stood with his arms crossed by the door to the small chapel. He, the priest, Jean, and the old seneschal—who'd waved happily to see her, but now stood quietly with Callan beside the tall windows—were the only witnesses. During her last wedding, the chapel and the steps had been packed with Mackenzies—

No.

No, she would not compare her weddings.

"No doubt he's been delayed," was all Jean offered.

Delayed? What could possibly have delayed him on his wedding day? He hadn't been among the small group to welcome her back to the Mackenzie holding; he hadn't been there when Callan had thrown himself at her and they'd hugged until she thought her ribs would snap. He hadn't been there when she'd come down from refreshing herself in her old chamber. And now she stood in front of the priest, with only an old woman for company.

Where *was* her bridegroom?

As if in answer, the heavy door swung open. Dougal stepped out of the way, but made no move to welcome the newcomer—he'd been in a grumpy mood since they'd left home. But Agata wasn't watching him; her eyes were on the man with his hand braced heavily on the door.

When he stepped away from it, she realized he'd been using it to hold himself upright. He stumbled into the aisle, paused, and righted himself. That's when she got the first good look at him, and knew this was her bridegroom.

Where David had been broad and blonde, Jaimie was tall and lithe, with long black hair. He wore the Mackenzie tartan, but it was rumpled, as if he'd donned it in the dark, or had fallen on his way to the chapel. And the way he stood, swaying in the aisle, caused his hair to fall in front of his face in greasy strands.

Agata swallowed, unsure if she was relieved he looked nothing like David or disgusted by his appearance.

Then Jaimie took a step, swayed further, and seemed in danger of falling. Without thinking, Agata hiked up her skirts and rushed toward him, intent on keeping him from falling on his face.

When she reached him, she instinctively clasped his forearm, to keep him upright. In doing so, her gaze landed on his hand.

As an artist, she'd always been intrigued by men's hands—so strong and powerful, holding so much potential. Jaimie's hand had a sprinkling of dark hairs across the back, and all four of his fingers ended above the third knuckle. As she stared down at it in confusion, he muttered a curse and curled his fingers and thumb into a fist.

To hide them from her? The thought made her stomach flip, hating to have caused him pain, and she loosened her hold on him to stroke her fingers along his forearm in comfort.

She might as well have branded him. With a snarl, her intended reared back, jerking away from her and turning horrified eyes on her, and she got her first real look at him.

He was hideous.

What had happened to cause such a scar across the left side of his face? It wasn't a burn and didn't appear to be a result of a disease. But the skin under his eye, across his cheek and back toward his ear and down his jaw was red and hard-looking. It almost appeared melted. It pulled his left eye down and made him look sadder.

But his eyes—the same dark blue David, Jean, and Callan shared—were full of anger as he glared at her.

With a gasp, she pulled her hand away from him, taking a step back altogether to allow him some space. After a moment, she watched his nostrils flare and his shoulders straighten as the fury in his gaze slowly dissipated. Fury? Because she'd touched him?

They hadn't been properly introduced, but they were to be married. Agata glanced toward the altar, where Jean stood, her hands clasped in front of her, a faint smile on her lips. If *she* wasn't going to do anything about this strange meeting, it was clear no one else was either. It was up to Agata.

Still holding the bunch of rosemary—for remembrance, she thought wryly—she dipped a curtsey. "Milord," she murmured, not dropping her eyes from his.

He was the one to look away first, the right side of his face flushing slightly as his tongue flicked out over his lower lip. "Lady Agata," he finally acknowledged, staring over her shoulder.

When he spoke, Agata smelled the spirits on his breath, and did her best not to recoil. He was drunk! He was drunk on their wedding day!

No wonder he was late.

For the first time, Agata wondered if Jaimie Mackenzie

wanted to be married to her. Why hadn't she thought to ask Jean that?

This marriage was the right thing for Agata; her arms ached to hold Callan again. But if her husband was against it from the start, would their alliance ever have a chance of success?

She swallowed, knowing she'd have to address this before they said their vows. But quietly, so Jean—and Dougal—couldn't overhear.

"Milord?" Suppressing her revulsion of his drunkenness, she leaned in closer, trying not to be offended when he leaned away from her. "Milord, are ye—are ye...?"

"Drunk?" he rasped. "Aye, frequently."

She frowned, and wondered if he'd intended to offend her. "Nay. I meant, is this alliance of yer choosing? Jean made the arrangements with my father, and I ken—"

To her surprise, he burst into laughter.

When the fumes rolled over her, she clamped her lips shut, part in disgust and part in humiliation.

His laughter wasn't nice. Nay, there was a desperate edge to it, and the longer it went on, the more uncomfortable she became. Jean didn't help; merely watched. Finally, Agata, irritated at being the butt of his humor and yet somehow aching to hear his attempts at merriment, snapped.

"Ye're laughing at yer bride, milord?"

He sobered instantly, swaying in place. "I'm laughing because my bride thinks to *save me* from our marriage. I'm laughing because I've fallen so low, I need a woman to fight my battles now."

The words sounded flippant, but there was a pain in those dark blue eyes which made her think they were the truth.

This man was nothing like David.

He hesitated where David was strong. He doubted where David was sure.

And despite Jaimie's apparent need to get drunk on his wedding day, despite the fumes coming off him, and the grease in his hair, seeing the pain in his eyes made him infinitely more appealing than David.

"I willnae fight yer battles for ye, Jaimie," she said gently. "But I will stand beside ye as ye fight them yerself."

Looking stunned, the man shook his head and looked away. Then, muttering a curse, he squeezed his eyes shut. "I'll marry ye willingly, lady. My aunt assures me 'tis for the best, and ye're not—"

When he growled and pressed his lips together, Agata found herself left wanting. She wasn't, what? *Suitable? Ugly? Undesirable?* Had he been about to insult her or compliment her?

They stood in the center of the chapel, their small audience looking on, but likely unable to hear what had passed between them. Agata's hands shook again, so she clasped the bouquet in front of her to keep from touching him.

To keep from comforting him when he obviously wanted no comfort from her.

"'Tis glad I am to hear it, milord," she murmured with a false smile. "Our marriage will be a strong match and good for our clans."

She paused, hoping he'd say something—*anything*—in agreement.

When he didn't, she forced herself to go on in an overly cheerful manner. "And after our journey of the last few days, I look forward to the wedding feast I'm sure Edward has arranged with the kitchens." She knew she was babbling now, but couldn't seem to make herself stop. "But I do hope ye'll bathe afore coming to my bed tonight, milord," she teased.

His eyes snapped to her once more, and the look in them made her step back in protection. Part rage, part hurt, part disgust—she'd made him feel all those with her careless words?

"There will be no bedding, lass," he growled, stepping toward her for the first time. He lowered his chin as he glared. "I'll marry ye, but dinnae expect me to bed ye."

Her heart slammed against her ribs at his unexpected declaration. Mayhap it was her surprise which emboldened her, because she shifted forward once more, until they were mere inches apart.

"Ye *will* bed me," she surprised herself by declaring. "As my husband, 'tis yer duty."

The right side of his lips curled as his nostrils flared. She didn't know what that expression meant, but from the look in his eyes, it wasn't good. "Ye dinnae ken what ye demand, woman."

Lifting the rosemary, she stopped herself just short of poking him in the chest with it, and instead, shook the fragrant herb under his nose. "I *do*. I was lady of this keep once afore, and I'll be again, Jaimie Mackenzie. Ye'll no' keep me from my rightful place."

Aye. Her rightful place. If he refused to bed her, refused to consummate the marriage, then she wouldn't really be lady of the keep. Their marriage alliance would keep the peace, but without consummation, it would ruin any chance she had of maintaining order in her home.

When he blinked, it was obvious he hadn't considered those ramifications. Now he looked...unsure. Did he doubt her? Or doubt her reasons?

Or did he doubt she wanted him to touch her?

Well, she'd endured David's touch. The marriage bed hadn't been pleasurable, but after the first few times, it wasn't horrible or painful either. Oh, she'd answered her sisters' questions, and knew how to bring herself to pleasure, but such frivolity hadn't mattered to David. How many nights had he grunted above her until the act was complete, then he left her to pray his seed would take root? How many nights had she been left aching and empty and alone because he'd cared nothing for her experience?

Well, after that, she could endure being bedded by Jaimie as well.

Sucking in a deep breath through her teeth, she straightened to her full height—although she still had to look up into his eyes—and thrust out her chin. "If ye marry me, Jaimie, ye'll bed me as well." Before he had time to respond—*if* he was going to respond—she gave him her shoulder. "If ye kneel afore Father Simon with me, ye're pledging to do both. And the decision is yers."

Without looking at him, she marched toward the altar, where the priest had been waiting patiently. With a nod to him and Jean, Agata sunk to her knees and forced a serene expression, as if nothing was wrong. As if her heart wasn't beating in terror. Would her gamble pay off?

Had she just ruined her chance at a future, her chance to find the jewels, her chance with *Callan* by making such a demand?

A million heartbeats seemed to pass, each breath harder than the last. Jean shifted impatiently, and Agata squeezed her eyes shut on a silent prayer.

Please God, dinnae let me die of embarrassment. Let me hug Callan as his mother again.

Maybe it was her prayer. Maybe the man had just seen sense. Either way, an eon later, Agata heard the rustle of fabric behind her, and her eyes flew open. With a grunt, her foul-smelling, bedraggled bridegroom sunk to his knees beside her, and nodded once to the priest.

"Get on with it," he muttered.

They weren't words of love or affection. It wasn't even heartening. But as Father Simon began to intone the blessing in Latin, Agata felt the tension around her heart ease in relief.

She was marrying the Mackenzie regent.

***

GOD'S BLOOD, but he was thirsty.

That blasted priest had droned on for what felt like an hour, and Jaimie had been near parched by the time the man had waved his hands for the final blessing. Then, Aunt Jean had hugged Jaimie and his bride, tears in her eyes, and dragged them to the great hall for the wedding feast.

When David had wed Aileen, Jaimie had made himself scarce, retreating to court for over four years. But even then, he assumed the wedding feast had been more festive than this one. Hell, a *funeral* would have been more festive.

Jaimie had sat in his brother's chair, one leg hooked over the arm and a cup of *uisge-beatha* in his hand, and watched his new wife preside over a subdued crowd. Subdued, that is, until Callan joined them.

"Agata!" the lad had squealed, the joy in his voice evident as his expression lit up. "Ye're back!"

And his bride had lit up as well.

He'd known she was beautiful. She *must* be, if David had consented to marry her. But coming face-to-face with her in that chapel had made Jaimie want to vomit. She wasn't just beautiful, she was…well, his muddled thoughts couldn't come up with anything better than *beautiful,* so that was that. But she was.

He took another gulp, appreciating the way it burned his throat on the way down.

She'd been beautiful, and he wasn't. Not anymore. He knew that, and had thought he'd come to terms with it. But when he'd realized she was looking at his ruined hands, and had responded not with revulsion, but with sympathy—at least, he assumed that's what her touch meant—he'd...

Jaimie hadn't realized he could still get so angry. He thought his anger had died the same night Aileen had. He thought he'd drowned it in self-pity.

He'd been wrong.

His bride had touched him with sympathy he hadn't deserved, and had no one to be angry with but himself.

Taking another gulp, he watched her on her knees in front of Callan, their arms wrapped around one another. Around them, the Mackenzies seemed to come alive, laughing and calling out toasts to the pair.

Had Aileen ever held her son with this much love? Did Callan remember his mother sharing affection this way?

"What?" the boy had yelled, pulling back and staring open-mouthed in Jaimie's direction. Had no one told him his uncle would be marrying his stepmother? Jaimie sure as hell hadn't —he avoided the boy as much as humanly possible.

God Almighty, what a mess.

The rest of the meal was better, sitting between Callan and Aunt Jean. Both thankfully ignored him, and the clan's merriment seemed to grow in proportion to his moroseness. Finally, it was time for Agata to retire upstairs to her chambers, which connected to David's old rooms.

Where Jaimie was supposed to join her.

He had muttered a curse and lifted his cup once more—then complained when it was pulled from his hand.

"Any more of that, lad, and ye'll be unable to fulfill yer duty." Jean's words had been light, but her eyes were hard as she shoved a piece of brown bread into his hands to replace the spirits. "Eat that. Soak up yer drink. And *join her.*"

So now he stood in the corridor in front of her door, his lips dry, and his throat parched. He'd decided against bathing, as she'd requested—nay, *commanded*—him to, because he'd not be ordered around like a child. But after that interminable wedding ceremony, Jaimie found himself headed toward the loch.

She was as spoiled and demanding as Aileen had been. But instead of punishing her, he was giving her exactly what she wanted.

Him. Sweeter-smelling and ready to bed his wife, if his cock was any assessment.

But still not sober.

Steeling himself, he stepped into her room. There was no crowd of giggling women, thank God. No one to witness an act which would be cold and meaningless.

Still, seeing her standing there in front of the open window, the breeze causing her robe to sway around her legs, made him hesitate. She really was beautiful, wasn't she? Not in a soft sense, the way Aileen had been. Agata had honey-colored hair and brown eyes he'd noticed had flashed between sable and gold. But her features were sharp, and she looked more like someone an ancient sculptor would have admired, rather than someone Jaimie would have chosen to warm his bed.

No, he preferred his women plump and willing to take coin. But this one was his wife now, and it wouldn't matter, because he wouldn't have to watch her anyhow.

Determined to do as she'd commanded, he reached for his belt. Once, long ago, he might've worn a weapon beside his knife, but he wasn't worthy anymore, so disrobing was easy. His kilt was loose and draped over one shoulder by the time he looked up.

She was staring at him, eyes wide, her hands clutched at her robe. He lifted his chin and one brow in challenge. Had she thought he'd fuck her in the dark? Had she thought he'd wait? To hell with that—he needed a drink badly, needed to get this over with.

"Well?" he growled.

To his surprise, she crossed the room to stop before him. She took a deep breath, then lifted her right hand. This close, he could see the flecks of gold in her eyes, see the determination and intention in them.

Which is why, faster than even he'd expected, he caught her wrist before her hand reached his cheek. His ruined fingers wrapped around her tender skin, and she flinched.

"Dinnae touch me," he rasped out, the warning clear. Over the years, he'd met more than a few lassies who'd been fascinated by the cold burns the winter had left him, and he'd told them the same thing. "I dinnae like to be touched."

"Everyone likes to be touched, Jaimie," she whispered in return, her eyes wide. Despite that flinch, there was no fear in her gaze.

And that bothered him more than he expected. God, he was thirsty.

His tongue darted out over his lip, and he wished his throat wasn't so dry. "Get on the bed."

When she turned her head to look at the piece of furniture he'd indicated, the long column of her throat stretched, and he could see the flicker of her pulse in the hollow at the base. The fast rhythm told him she was nervous, but rather than feeling vindicated, he was nigh overwhelmed with the desire to *taste* her there.

The desire to pull her into his arms, to press his lips to the honey-cream skin of her neck, to close his hand around one of the perfect breasts he was sure hid beneath that nightrail of hers. He wanted to *touch* her, to *taste* her. To feel her all around him.

His cock went hard behind the drape of his plaid.

She took a deep breath—he didn't even bother trying to hide the fact he'd stared at the way her large breasts strained against her chemise—and turned toward the bed. With her back to him, she removed the robe and draped it over the foot of the bed, then turned to sit on the edge. Another deep breath told him she might be nervous as she scooted backward.

His pulse was pounding under his jaw as he watched, surprised by how quickly his body had jumped at the knowledge of what was coming. In the last years since Aileen's death, he'd only taken a woman when his hand would no longer do. Even then, he hadn't *bedded* the whores.

Agata was his *wife*.

Still, when she'd reached the center of the bed, laid back, and began inching the hemline of her nightrail up, he held up his hand to stop her.

"Flip over," he growled.

Her movements halted, the creamy linen lying against the perfect skin above her knees, and Jaimie felt his cock thrum with the need to feel her there.

"What?" she croaked out.

"Flip over," he repeated, pulling his plaid off his shoulder and tossing it over a nearby chair. "So we can consummate this damned marriage."

"Flip…over?" Her brows dipped, but he wasn't sure if it was anger or confusion. "As in, ye want me on my stomach?"

He shrugged, and reached under his shirt to stroke himself. "Or on yer knees, with yer arse in the air. I care no'."

Now her eyes narrowed, and—God in heaven!—was she a sight when riled. Or maybe it was just because he hadn't buried his cock in a woman in a long while. He stroked himself again.

"Nay," she finally said, and resumed the sweet torture of lifting her chemise. "I think ye *do* care."

"Ye think wrong," he snapped.

From her spot on the bed, she merely shrugged, and paused with the linen barely covering her mound. "I'm yer wife, and I'll no' be taken like a hound bitch."

Had she defied David this way? Did she see Jaimie as a weak man, a man she could order about?

Maybe she was right.

He shrugged, pretending he wasn't bothered. "'Tis for yer own good."

So she didn't have to watch him as he thrust into her. So she didn't have to pretend not to grimace as she was taken by a monster.

And maybe she realized that, because her chin came up and she lifted her arse just enough to pull her chemise up all the way. The linen rested against her flat belly, hiding what he knew were her perfect breasts, and framing her round hips.

She lifted her knees, planted her heels on the bed, and spread her legs.

Had Jaimie thought this throat dry before? God in heaven, he could barely *breathe* now.

His strokes coming swifter as he stepped up beside the bed. Despite what he'd told her about touching him, he *ached* with the need to put his hands on her, to run his hands along her skin, to have her caress him the way she had in the chapel. He needed to taste her, to smell her musky perfection… but he wouldn't. He was no longer that man.

Instead, he tugged at his own cock, his gaze raking her legs and mound, knowing he'd spill as soon as he was sheathed inside. And he'd do it, whether she was staring at his scars or not.

With a snarl, he wrapped his ruined hands around her ankles and yanked her toward him. The movement spoiled her careful tease with the chemise, and the material ended up bunched up under her breasts. His palms itched to cup them, to fondle them, but he knew her look of revulsion would be one which would cut him deeply, so he didn't.

Instead, he met her eyes in challenge. *This is what ye wanted,* he almost said. *Ye could've turned over, but now ye'll have to watch a monster pumping into ye.*

It would serve the little tyrant right.

He flipped up the end of his shirt, and his cock leapt as the air brushed against it. Her eyes widened, but she didn't look away. Crudely, he lifted his thumb to his mouth and rasped his tongue along it, wetting it. Before she could guess his intent, he'd reached forward and dragged it through her slit.

She bucked under him, but he wasn't sure if it was because of the unexpected move or because it felt good. A pang of guilt made him shudder as he remembered the ecstasy he used to bring women to, but he pushed it aside.

And then, taking a hold of himself once more, he stepped into the circle of her legs and pushed into her.

She sucked in a breath as her tightness clamped around him. She wasn't dry, but wasn't as wet as she should be, and he felt another pang of guilt over that.

To hell with guilt! This marriage—this bedding!—wasn't his idea in the first place. With a growl, he grabbed her knees and began working in her.

The rhythm should've comforted him, should've soothed him. But the closer he came to release, the more disturbed he became.

Because she wasn't reacting. Wasn't panting in pleasure the way his old lovers had. Wasn't turning away with her eyes closed on a resigned wince, the way his new lovers did. Nay, she was…she was *watching* him, her expression curiously blank.

And aye, the more he thrust into her tightness, the wetter she became, but that wasn't *passion*. It wasn't *right*.

Still, he was only a man, and her wetness grasped at his cock as he felt the familiar pressure build at its base. Maybe his rhythm had changed. Maybe his expression did. Either way, when he felt he was close, she did the damnedest thing.

She *smiled* at him. As if welcoming him. As if knowing he was just *using* her body and *approved* of it.

And God help him, that knowledge sent him over the edge. For the first time since she'd climbed on the bed, he broke eye contact with her, throwing back his head with a wordless bellow of release as he spilled his seed deep inside her.

It felt...

It felt good. He rocked against her slickness, made slicker still, and felt his blood thumping against the base of his brain and *knew* he'd been a complete arse. He panted and stared at the bed's curtains, trying to drag his body under control. He slumped, his strength giving out at the same moment he'd realized how futile the effort was, and planted his fists on either side of her hips as he tried to calm his breathing.

He was staring down at her perfect navel, wondering what in the hell had just happened, when he saw her lift her hand. And before he could stop her, before he could utter the obvious lie of not liking to be touched, her fingertips skimmed against the ruined skin of his cheek.

Jaimie flinched away, but didn't manage to go far. And it didn't seem to matter, because she hadn't intended to touch him there. No, instead, her fingers merely swept across his skin, lifting his hair away from the scar and tucking it behind his ear.

And once she'd completed such an intimate, tender action, her lips lifted in another sweet smile.

The shock of it slammed into his chest, knocking him away from her. As he stumbled back, he slid out of her, severing whatever brief connection they might have shared. He staggered away from the bed, his shirt falling to cover him once more, and his hand rising to press against his ruined face as he stared at her with shock.

Who *was* this woman, to touch him so?

More shaken than he could admit, Jaimie fumbled for his

plaid, angry at the way his hands trembled as he tried to wrap it.

Nay! She was just a lass, just a wench in his bed. There was no reason for him to feel so dazed by her… was there? Wife or no, she'd not be bothering him again to do his duty by her.

He lurched for the door, leaning heavily on it as he turned against his better judgement. She was propped on her elbows, and her expression…

She looked *disappointed*.

He cursed and yanked open the door, unnerved by what she'd done to him.

I need a drink.

CHAPTER 4

"Did ye miss this?"

She and Callan were standing on one of the rises over-looking Mackenzie land, the keep at their back and the mountains and valley before them. The boy's question drew her attention from the stunning view.

She smiled down at the boy. "Aye," she admitted. "'Tis impossible not to be awed by this view." She winked. "But even more, I missed having *ye* to share it with."

At her confession, the boy's face lit up, and her heart clenched at the sight. She'd missed him so much, missed *this* so much. Missed being with him, missed sharing what she loved with him.

And while this might not have been the return she'd long dreamed of, at least they were together once more.

She couldn't even regret being married to the boy's uncle. Jaimie was *nothing* like David. And even though he appeared, at first meeting, to be a man she never would have chosen for her husband... she couldn't deny he was compelling. Intriguing.

Certainly, his drunkenness was unappealing, but even she,

who had just met him, could see how hurt he was. Not physically, because his scars had long since healed, but inside. He'd been hurt, and was still hurting.

And although she didn't have her sister Pearl's healing skills, Agata ached to heal him.

She'd never ran from a challenge, and didn't intend to now. The man was her husband, and she could see he was so much more than the shell-of-a-human she'd married yesterday.

"So, when are we coming back out wi' our paints?"

She realized she'd been staring at the mountains while she thought about Jaimie, but Callan's question yanked her back to this sunny hillside.

"Ye still have yer paints?"

"Aye, of course," the boy said factually. "With Father gone, there was nae one to disapprove. I've even made a few of my own."

Although her lips tugged down at the memory of David's casual cruelty, Agata forced herself to focus on the pride in the boy's words. "Really? What pigments have ye used?

His hand still in hers, Callan shrugged. "Mostly browns, 'cause they're easiest. I remember how ye had that one from far away."

"Burnt sienna from Italy," she supplied.

He shrugged. "Aye, but I've mainly just been using dirt."

"That's because ye're brilliant. Burnt sienna is just dirt they've cooked and crumbled." Tugging on his hand, she directed his attention back to the sight before them. "Ye see that mountain to the south?"

"Aye! That's where our treasure is, Lady Jean says."

Agata chuckled at his interpretation of the Mackenzie saying. "Well, if we had yer paints here, how would ye use yer new color?"

She watched him examine the view, and loved the way his little mouth pulled down into a frown. He was so serious, this once-stepson of hers, and she loved him for it. Seeing him yesterday had made her heart leap with joy, for he'd grown so much in the months they'd been parted. Although David had been blonde, Callan's mother had been as dark as Jaimie. Callan's dark hair and Mackenzie-blue eyes made him look very much like his uncle.

Callan wasn't much like David, and she loved him all the more for it. She loved the way he examined everything so thoroughly before making decisions, loved his intense emotions, and loved how thoughtful and sensitive he could be, despite his father's best efforts to make him hard and unfeeling.

In the short time she'd been here and been the lad's step-mother, she'd done everything possible to encourage his introspection and expression, against David's wishes.

Finally, Callan hummed thoughtfully. "'Tis summertime, so the valley is more green than brown. I suppose I could use my pigment wi' some gray, over there for those rocks." Using his free hand, he pointed toward the boulders at the base of the mountain.

She nodded in approval. "And how would we make that gray?"

"Soot and lead white," the boy answered promptly.

Her pride wrenched a laugh from her lips. "Good! Aye, that's how we do it. What other colors would we need if we painted this scene?"

Callan nodded toward the mountain. "More gray and blues, but ye dinnae like to use blue, do ye?"

She shook her head, agreeing with him. "'Tis too expensive. The azurite has to come all the way from Germany, so it's easier to use malachite."

"But that's green!"

She was impressed he remembered. "Aye! But sometimes malachite can be found in shades of blue, as well."

Her stomach growled then, reminding her how long they'd been out here enjoying the natural grace of the land. With the sun past its zenith, she and Callan would be missed... especially on today, her first day as the lady of the keep.

When she tugged gently on his hand, the boy turned almost reluctantly away from the view, and that made her smile. She continued her earlier lecture, in an attempt to distract him.

"Although I've never used it, the most beautiful blue, the pure blue we so often see on the Virgin Mary's wimple, is made from lapis lazuli."

"Lapi...?" The boy attempted the name.

"Lapis lazuli," she said again, enunciating the syllables so he could learn the words. "'Tis a beautiful blue stone which comes from a land far to the east and south."

"England?"

Hiding her grin, Agata shook her head, knowing that even with the recent conflicts with England, that country was still very far away in Callan's mind.

"Nay, much farther than England. Beyond France and Italy and the empire. 'Tis why it's so valuable, and why depictions of our Lord's sainted mother are one of the few allowed to use such a color."

The boy grunted and kicked a stone out of their way as they reached the footpath. "Ye once let me use yer blue, but I don't remember what it was."

"Azurite, as I recall. But painting the mountain gray is much easier."

"Aye! I liked last summer when ye showed me how to use green wi' dots of color to paint the meadow. I still have that painting."

"That's because the wood we painted on will last a while. Remember I told ye how verdigris is made? But that green tends to eat through parchment, because of the copper it's made from."

That led to a discussion of distilling and alchemy, which apparently interested Callan very much. She did her best to answer his questions, although she'd always purchased her verdigris and lead white pigments, because making them involved more steps than she was willing to attempt. But she knew the basic principles—suspending the copper or lead over vinegar, sealing the vase, and burying it, then coming back in a month to scrape off the pigments—and shared what she knew.

Although she knew more of painting than weaving, when Callan asked a question about a hue in one of the tapestries in the great hall, she tried to remember what she knew of dyeing and colors. But that reminded her of her reason for being here.

"Have ye ever seen any tapestries in the keep with the name Sinclair on them?"

If the boy thought the question odd, he didn't let on. Instead, he just shook his head and kicked at another stone, his sweaty little hand tucked in hers. "Why?"

She shrugged. If the ancient tapestry at home had the Mackenzie name woven into the strands, she'd wondered if the next clue to the jewels' whereabouts would be as simple to find here.

"Have ye ever seen *any* piece of Sinclair history here? A carving? Or maybe a circle with four smaller circles inside of it?"

"Nay, ye're the only Sinclair I've heard of! Did ye ask Lady Jean?"

She hid her wince. Nay, she hadn't revealed her quest to her aunt-by-marriage, anymore than she would explain her true purpose to the seven-year-old. She'd sworn not to share the purpose behind their hunt, and although it'd be easier with allies who knew the keep, she was sworn to secrecy.

Still, she had to answer the boy. "Why should I ask her?" she teased, "when I happen to be walking with the keep's best guide. Have ye noticed aught like that in yer explorations of the secret passages?"

It was almost sweet the way the lad's cheeks flushed guiltily. When he pulled his hand from hers, she knew he was nervous.

"I dinnae—I mean, the passages arenae…"

When he trailed off, she smiled and ruffled his hair. "As long as ye're careful in them, Callan, ye have every right to explore yer home. Ye'll be laird someday, ye ken."

He brightened at that, and nodded happily. "Ye're right! I'm practically laird now, Edward says. Although he only says that when I've done something foolhardy."

"Ye? Doing something foolhardy?" she asked incredulously, laughing. "I dinnae believe it!"

"Oh, aye!" he said with enthusiasm as he reached for her hand once more and began to swing it. "One time…"

Soon, she was laughing as hard as he was, as impressed by the schemes he'd come up with to torment his tutors as she'd been by his thought-provoking questions about alchemy. She was thrilled to have this discussion with him.

Truthfully, she was thrilled to have *any* discussion with him, much less one which revealed his intelligence and thoughtfulness. But as they approached the keep, Agata had to admit the truth, as much as she adored spending time with Callan, part of her had used the lad as a distraction. On this day, the first day of her new marriage, she should've been with her husband. But the idea of seeing him after what they'd shared last night, had made her too nervous.

Sitting on the dais yesterday during the wedding feast had reminded her of meals beside David. Her husband—her *first* husband—didn't speak to her either. But Jaimie had spoken to no one, and no one had spoken to him. Agata had spent most of the meal trying to think of a way to draw him into the lively discussions around him.

It hadn't worked, but at least it had distracted her from thinking about what was to come.

Yesterday evening, when he'd come to her room, she'd seen *hunger* in his eyes. A hunger she'd never seen from David, although Jaimie apparently had no intention of acting on it. He'd approached her as cold as his elder brother ever had, but his demand had taken her aback.

She was no blushing virgin. Her beddings by David had been as dispassionate and planned as everything in his life. He'd come to her room, gesture to her to hoist up her gown, enter her, and be done in minutes. She'd never forget that feeling of *emptiness*, when he'd adjust his clothes once more and leave her, spread and seeping, on the bed.

Nay, she was no virgin. But she knew there *must* be more to bedsport than what David had taught her. And when Jaimie had demanded she lie on her stomach, she'd thought he would teach her what she longed to know.

Until she'd seen the look in his eyes. Although the scarring on his face pulled his expression, his eyes were more haunted than any she'd ever seen. In that moment, she'd realized he'd made that demand of her, not because he was planning some passionate encounter, but so he wouldn't have to look at her.

Or she wouldn't have to look at him.

She'd made her decision to defy him then, to prove she was no longer the same woman who'd been married to David. She was stronger now, surer of herself. And she'd be strong enough for Jaimie, too.

Their mating had been like her other experiences, except for a moment at the beginning. Jaimie had cared enough to ensure she was slick before he entered her. David had never bothered, and her body had quickly become used to accommodating his. But when Jaimie had licked his finger and pressed it into her, the brush against Agata's already sensitive slit had sent her nearly off the bed. The sensation alone was new and exciting, but so was the knowledge he'd cared.

And then, when he'd found his release…

Agata swallowed, remembering the way her heart had pounded in her throat as she'd watched him looming over her, working in her. David had never met her eyes while he'd taken her, and his release was as restrained as he was. But Jaimie… Jaimie had *shouted*. He'd lost his control as he spilled his seed, and in that moment, Agata had never felt so powerful.

She wanted—*needed*—to touch him. To hold him, to be held. So, when he'd wrenched away from her like that, as if she'd burned him, her heart had sunk into her stomach. Remembering the lonely evenings after David had finished with her, Agata had spent her first night back as Lady Mackenzie curled on her side in her bed, praying for a baby to love.

Her reaction to Jaimie continued to disturb her.

She had Callan. She didn't need her new husband's affections, and certainly didn't need to *help* the man. So why did his pain cut her so deeply?

Beside her, Callan made a little noise of confusion. Her attention snapped to him, then in the direction he was gazing.

"What is it?" she prompted him.

"I've just…" He shook his head. "I've never seen him outside."

Never seen—? What is he talking about—

Oh.

There was a figure seated on a boulder just outside the village. His plaid was crooked and his elbows were braced on his knees. His head was in his palms, his hair falling in a curtain, and as they approached, Agata knew this was her husband.

He never ventured beyond the castle walls? Or had Callan meant exactly what he'd said, that Jaimie wasn't seen outside?

When they were nigh upon him, Callan called out, "Milord? Are ye well?"

Like lightening, the man thrust himself to his feet and tried to hide his wince. Did his head hurt? Or was it the sunlight?

But he was in no mood to be polite, apparently. "What are ye doing out here?"

Callan flinched. "We—we used to go for walks together, me an' Lady Agata."

How dare he make the boy feel guilty for taking his pleasure. Agata squeezed his hand and straightened her shoulders, determined in this newfound courage she'd found.

"If ye would snap at anyone, milord, blame me. I've missed Callan, and sought a few moments of peace with him. I lost track of time, and I apologize."

His blue eyes had gone to hers as she'd started to speak, but then quickly focused over her shoulder. Why? Did he not want to meet her gaze?

"Ye have half the keep looking for ye," he muttered.

"Jean kenned where we were," she shot back. "Did anyone think to ask her, milord?"

He frowned as his eyes darted back to hers, then away once more. "Enough with the 'milord,' both of ye. I have a name."

Aye, and she'd noticed he'd flinched last night when she'd used it. "Lord Jaimie—"

There! He'd flinched again before lifting his palm to cut her off. "Just Jaimie. And ye"—he pointed one stunted finger at the lad—"I'm yer uncle."

Callan was obviously confused by the man's censure. "Aye, milord uncle. Lady Jean says—"

"God Almighty, lad!" Jaimie threw his hands up in exasperation and turned on one booted heel to face the keep. "Just Uncle will do. And Agata is yer *aunt*—call her Aunt Agata," he finished in a mutter.

Baffled now, Callan turned his worried gaze to her. Agata smiled gently down at him, inordinately pleased to see her new husband apparently had a heart.

Squeezing his hand, she explained to the boy. "Yer Uncle Jaimie is saying there's no need to be so formal. Ye used to call me Lady Agata when I was married to yer father, but now that I'm married to yer uncle, I've become yer aunt."

"But my father said…"

When the boy trailed off, Agata nodded. "Yer father was… very certain of his way of doing things," she finished diplomatically. "But yer uncle is in charge now, 'til ye come of age. And I'm here as well."

Callan cocked his head as he watched her. "Ye're different now."

She nodded. *Aye*, she was different. Stronger, she hoped. "Yer father is gone, Callan, so that means I'm able to speak my mind." She squeezed his hand once more. "We *all* are. We can do the things *we* think are best now, aye?"

When her new husband snorted, she lifted her chin and raised one brow in defiance. His back was still to them, but she wasn't going to back down.

"Ye disagree, *husband*?"

Her lips twitched at the challenge she heard in her own voice. She'd learned that from Citrine, undoubtably. But last year, she would have never been so brave as to question David this way. As Callan had said, she was different.

Jaimie didn't respond, but his hands clenched into fists by his side, so she moved up beside him, pulling the lad with her.

"Ye think I shouldnae do what I think is best, husband?"

"I think ye'll do what ye think is best nae matter what," he growled, not looking at her. "I think ye expect to lead me around on a leash." A flicker of anger showed as he glanced at her, then away. "Like a *hound bitch.*"

The memory of last night made her cheeks heat, but she wasn't sure if he was teasing her or mocking her. Either way, her chin went up even further. "'Tis my duty as Lady Mackenzie to use my influence to the betterment of my clan and my family. That means doing what I can to ensure the right decisions are made."

"About what?"

"About ye."

She wasn't sure where that response had come from, but when he turned an incredulous expression her way, she didn't allow herself to hesitate or back down. She'd changed, and wouldn't be intimidated now.

Even if his smoldering glare *was* intimidating. At least it wasn't David's iciness.

"What's wrong with me?" he growled.

She opened her mouth to respond, then reconsidered. If she answered, it would prove she'd considered this already, and that would be a poor confession to begin her marriage with. Pressing her lips together, she considered how to reply.

Callan beat her to it. "Ye drink too much."

Both adults turned surprised gazes to the boy, who flushed, but straightened his shoulders and tightened his hold on Agata's hand.

"'Tis true," he said with a nod. "Lady—I mean, Aunt Jean thinks so, too. Ye drink too much."

Jaimie narrowed his eyes at the lad, then lifted his frowning expression to Agata. She didn't want to hurt him further, but she had to support Callan in this. She nodded firmly.

"'Tis true," she said gently. "I've kenned ye a short time, but yer reliance on the drink—"

"I dinnae rely on it," he snapped.

"Prove it," she snapped right back.

He blinked in surprise. "*Prove it?*" he repeated. "How?"

He was asking her advice! Oh, he might not realize that's what he was doing, but Agata leaped at the chance to help him. Schooling her features carefully, she made sure no pity entered her tone as she explained.

"Some men who've gone through much in their lives, turn to ale or spirits to drown—" *their pain.* But she wasn't sure if Jaimie would admit to his pain. "Their troubles," she substituted instead. "The more they drink, the more they come to rely on it. One drink isnae enough, then two, then ten. They always thirst for more."

She watched his tongue scrape across his lower lip. In a nervous gesture, or had her words made him thirsty? She pressed on, as gently as possible.

"A man like that, he becomes useless, Jaimie. He only lives for the drink, and everything—his honor, his clan, his responsibilities, his *family*—are forgotten."

He was staring at her now, and her heart ached at the hesitation she saw in his eyes. He was unsure, and she hated she'd been the one to cause that reaction in him. But it was a reaction, and that was better than nothing.

"Do ye..." He cleared his throat and tried again. "Do ye ken any men like that?"

I'm looking at one right now. But she wasn't certain Jaimie was that far gone. So, she just dropped her chin in a small nod.

"Aye. But I ken it can be fought, as well."

This time the question came from Callan. "How?"

Agata didn't dare glance down at him. She didn't dare drop Jaimie's gaze, for fear she'd lose the ground she'd gained with him.

"With determination," she answered the lad softly, but speaking to Jaimie. "It requires the man to *want* to fight it. Nae matter how hard his family and friends want him back, he has to want to get better. To defy the drink."

Jaimie stood there in the warm summer sun, his lithe and sunken frame attesting to how he'd ignored so much of life in recent years. Why? What had caused this decline? David had always spoken of his younger brother as a diplomat and courtier, but hadn't mentioned this dependence and desperation. Therefore, it was easy to surmise Jaimie hadn't always been like this.

He seemed to be considering her words as he studied her. When he hesitated, then swallowed, he seemed so lost. But he stared at her with... with *hope*.

And that's when she knew she would do anything to help this husband of hers.

"How does... how would a man fight the drink?" he rasped.

"With support from his friends and family," she immediately answered, praying he was willing to fight. "It takes days to sweat it out of his body, and even longer still to overcome its hold on his mind. He must find something to replace it in his heart."

His tongue dragged across his lower lip again as she described the ordeal. But he seemed to be considering her words. "Like what?"

For the first time, she allowed herself a smile. Not a proud one, but a small, soft smile. For him.

"Like his new wife, mayhap," she offered gently.

He reared back, shaking his head. In shock? In denial? With her heart pounding, Agata held her breath as tightly as she held Callan's hand.

Merciful Mother of Christ, help him see reason. Help him find the strength.

Jaimie was breathing hard when he met her eyes, and shook his head once more.

She held his gaze, allowed him to see her compassion and determination, and nodded.

Callan chose that moment to pull away from her, maybe not understanding the decision his uncle faced. With a cry of welcome, he ran toward a group of lads heading toward the loch, and dimly, Agata thought to remind him of his manners.

But the damage had been done. When she turned back from his distraction, Jaimie's gaze was hooded once more. He now looked wary, rather than desperate or hopeful.

She swallowed down her disappointment. "He loves ye, ye ken," she offered. "'Tis obvious by his worry."

Jaimie scoffed and turned away. "He's his father's son," he bit out as his long legs ate up the distance to the keep.

She hurried to catch up, determined not to be left behind. "And his mother's," she reminded him.

He snorted and shook his head so wildly his hair flew around his face. "'Tis no compliment, that."

She'd never met David's first wife, but stories from Jean and the seneschal hadn't painted the woman well. So she shrugged.

"Mayhap. But ye're his family now. And so am I." She was panting to keep up. "And I think a lad like him needs to ken 'tis fine to show his emotions like that, aye?"

With that, she reached over and touched Jaimie's arm, the same way she had yesterday in the chapel. And just like yesterday, he flinched away… but at least he halted.

When she moved to stand in front of him, she saw the way he dropped his gaze to her hands. Last night he'd said he didn't like to be touched, but that *had* to be a lie. The way he'd responded to his climax told her he wasn't as restrained as he pretended to be.

"Is that no' right, Jaimie," she prompted softly. "'Tis important for a child to ken it's acceptable to *feel*. To be loud and talented and love as hard as possible." *Not* like David would've raised him.

Jaimie blew out a breath and dropped his head back to stare at the top-most tower of the keep. She wondered what he saw there. At long last, he closed his eyes on a muttered, "Aye. 'Tis best for Callan."

"And he does love ye, ye ken." She didn't dare touch him again, but her hand itched to reach for his, to urge him to make the right choice, even if he didn't realize a choice was being made. "He deserves to ken ye love him as well."

She held her breath, praying he wouldn't deny his feelings for the lad. Praying he *had* feelings for the lad, and his obvious dislike of Aileen hadn't darkened his opinion of the boy.

Finally, he exhaled and twisted toward the loch. When he did, his hair fell away from his scarred cheek, and the reflected sunlight caught in his blue eyes. In that moment, she saw him as the man he'd once been—the man he might be again. *Strong. Sure of himself. Beautiful.*

Her attention was caught by the pulse ticking under his jaw, as he clenched those muscles. He was thinking, considering her words, and her heart soared with that knowledge. Her sisters had always told her she was the most level-headed of them all, the most logical. Her marriage to David, however, had taught her that a man didn't want and would never listen to her advice.

Mayhap this one was different. Mayhap *Jaimie* was different.

"I do," he said softly. "I've never told him. I avoid him."

Why? The urge to ask was nigh overwhelming, but she dug her fingernails into her palms and just nodded encouragingly. "Will ye tell him?"

"He deserves to ken it." Jaimie swallowed again. "He deserves a happy home."

"He deserves a family. An uncle he can look up to."

Holding her breath once more, she prayed he'd realize what she was saying.

When he turned to her, that cautious hope once more in his eyes, she knew God had granted her the response she'd asked for.

"Will ye—will ye help me?" he rasped out. "Will ye help me fight the drink?"

And in that moment, Agata knew her reason for being here among the Mackenzies. She might have accepted her father's decision as a way to be close to Callan again, and a way to search for the jewels. But now that she was here, she had one purpose, to help this man regain himself.

She smiled gently as she agreed. "Aye, Jaimie, I'd be honored."

CHAPTER 5

The fog was lifting.

Jaimie felt as if he was coming out of a dream, a vague dream of the last three years. Everything was…*hazy*. But now, today, he could see and think clearer than he had in a long while.

Maybe it was the hot water of the bath he soaked in. Maybe it was the cool breeze through the window. Maybe it was *her*.

There'd been times in the last fortnight—or had it been longer?—when Jaimie had outright hated the woman. His new *wife* had seemed to derive real pleasure from torturing him, but after what he'd put her through on their wedding night, he likely deserved it. She'd gotten her revenge well enough; forcing water down his throat, nagging him until he'd eaten enough of the thick brown bread the chatelaine had sent up, and—God help him!—talking to him.

She'd insisted on moving him here, to David's chambers, so she could be near him. And in the long days Jaimie spent writhing on the bed, or vomiting in the pot, or shivering under a fine sheen of sweat, she stood by, talking to him.

Telling him about the most mundane things, like how Callan's lessons were going or how many times the boy hit the target with his new bow. Or the changes she'd like to make in the great hall or tapestries she wanted moved. Or how her strange alchemy with pigments and dyes magically turned into painted masterpieces.

Although Jaimie had lost count of the days, he knew there was one morning she and Callan had even set up easels in the laird's chambers and happily chattered as they painted, oblivious to Jaimie's torment across the room.

He sighed and sunk lower in the water. Aye, she tortured him these last days. But he had to admit, she cared for him better than a man like him could ever hope. She'd been there to wipe his brow, to hold the bucket, and to ensure he ate something. And whenever he'd beg for more ale, she talked to him instead.

Now, as the fog was lifting from around his mind, Jaimie realized the truth; she hadn't been chattering mindlessly. No, she'd been giving him something to focus on, something to care about. By involving Callan, she reminded him why he was doing this in the first place.

He closed his eyes and rested his head on the edge of the tub. Aye, it would've been easier to go on in a fog, letting the drink control his life. But the day after his wedding, seeing Callan's concern for him... it had been enough to force a change in Jaimie. He'd thought about how hard and unbending David and their father had been. He'd thought about how Callan, God love him, was as open and loving as Jaimie had once been, despite David's best efforts to crush that side of his personality.

And Jaimie had known what he had to do.

Callan was his responsibility now, and he had to ensure the boy was raised to know it was acceptable to *feel* and to show those feelings. But the path Jaimie had been on wouldn't allow him to *raise* anyone. He'd been heading for a grave, either because of his own neglect or an ale-induced accident. If he died, the same as David, Agata would go back home again and Callan would be left with no one.

So, he'd made the decision to fight, and God forgive him, it'd been worse than the days following the winter burns.

But now…

He shifted lower in the tub, dunking his head under altogether and soaking his hair, before he eased to the surface once more.

This wasn't his first bath in the last week. His new wife seemed to have all sorts of opinions about what was good for a man in the throes of torment, and hot baths to leech out the infection was one of them. Of course, she'd been standing by with cold compresses as well, to wipe away the sweat which had made him shiver, and to whisper reassurances. That had been oddly encouraging, to hear that she was proud of him.

It had made the torture easier to bear.

Tonight, though, she'd directed the servants to bring in the tub, had poured in some kind of sweet-smelling oil, and opened the shutters on the large windows.

"Enjoy yer bath, husband," she'd murmured with a smile, before slipping through the door to her connecting chamber.

Five years ago, he wouldn't have called himself a weak man. But after what he'd just gone through, after what he was realizing he'd put himself through over the last years of drink-induced stupor, Jaimie decided that being ordered around by his wife wasn't the worst thing in the world. Her strength, her *surety*, gave him an anchor, something to rely on when he needed it most.

Besides, one thing he'd learned over the last days was that she might be stubborn and opinionated, but she was usually right.

And again, in this case, she was. The bath was as near to

divine as he could remember. Well, the pleasure of a woman's arms around him, of her smile as she called out his name… *that* would be divine. But he hadn't experienced that in long years, and here and now, this hot bath was close enough.

Through the window, the sun was sinking low in the west, and a fresh summer breeze blew through the chamber. His wife had aired out the room, changed the rushes, and placed flowers around, so it was as pleasing to the nose as to the eye, and now those scents brushed across his senses. The combination of the steam from the bath and the cool breeze made him grin in pleasure.

For a woman who'd been forced upon him by an overbearing aunt, then spent the first weeks of their marriage torturing him, Agata Sinclair was bringing him a surprising amount of pleasure.

Agata and pleasure? That thought led to another, and he felt himself growing hard under the water. She'd shown no interest in sharing his bed, but why would she? On their wedding night, he'd taken her like the monster he was, and since then, she'd seen him at his most disgusting.

But still, he couldn't forget the sight of her, spread out on her bed like some kind of feast. A feast just for him. Her smooth legs, her tight sheath… his cock leapt at the memory, and Jaimie dropped one hand to stroke himself. Despite the heat of the water, he was rock-hard, so he closed his eyes and rested his head against the edge of the tub and remembered the way her body had felt, gripping his.

His tongue darted out over his lower lip, imagining what she would *taste* like. She was the first woman in years to meet his gaze so boldly as she took him into herself. He tightened his ruined fingers around himself as he stroked, remembering the way she'd looked at him. Gently, intensely. As if she'd been *glad* to be fucked by him.

This wife of his, the woman who'd once been David's, was intriguing.

God Almighty, but it had felt good to lose himself in her, to feel her close around his cock that way. He pumped harder, the familiar pressure building behind his bollocks. She'd taken him—taken *all* of him, it had felt like—and then *smiled* when he'd spilled inside her. What would it feel like to lower himself atop her? To take her breast in his mouth? To brush the skin of his cheek against her stomach, to inhale her scent? To skim his palm across her hips and over her curls?

To sink into her once more?

Jaimie's breaths were coming faster as he stroked himself closer to completion, picturing his wife spread out for him once more. Blindly, he groped for one of the cloths stacked on the chair beside the tub, knowing he would put it to use for what it hadn't been intended for.

As he dragged the cloth into the water, he pictured another use for it, to wash *her*. If she were here in this tub with him right now, he'd pull her down atop him, not caring how much water they spilled over the edge. As she lowered herself onto his cock, she'd be smiling into his eyes again, and he'd use the cloth and the soap to lather her smooth skin until she squirmed.

The thought of having her on top of him, her large breasts level with his mouth, was what set Jaimie over. He closed the cloth around his cock, arched his back, and spilled his seed with a groan.

God in heaven.

He was still panting when he opened his eyes and stared at the distant sunset. He wadded up the wet cloth and tossed it over the side of the tub, then flexed his fingers. For the first time in a long time, he felt… caged. God, he should be wiped out by that climax, but instead, he wanted to run, to get outside, to enjoy the summer evening.

And maybe he would have if the door to her chamber hadn't opened at that moment.

He swallowed and lowered himself into the tub once more, thanking God she hadn't come in a minute ago. Or would that have been a good thing, to have her there as he stroked himself? The question brought a little smile to his lips as he watched her move about the room.

"Yer bath seems to have agreed with ye, Jaimie," she said in a pleased voice.

Jaimie. He'd told her to call him that, rather than the ridiculous "milord." And while Aileen used to say his name cajolingly, connivingly, it sounded like a blessing on Agata's lips.

And he couldn't deny she was right. "Aye," he all but sighed, sinking down into the warm water once again. His stomach still clenched at the thought of climbing out of the tub, of doing something wild, of really *living*... but at the same moment, he felt his earlier energy slipping away into a languid lethargy. It was pleasant to lie here in the water, to watch her putting away signs of his infirmity, making things right again.

"Heat is just the thing to leech out the last of the poisons," she said, her back to him as she arranged a shelf to her satisfaction. "Ye should be up and about in no time."

He'd been *up* mere moments ago, but he was certainly feeling *leeched* now. "Aye," he agreed again. "Mayhap I'll go fer a ride tomorrow."

"A ride?" She was smiling as she turned to him. "That sounds lovely. Might Callan and I join you?"

Lovely. His eyes raked her, impressed by how good she looked with the Mackenzie plaid crossing her heart. Did she ride as well as she painted?

His nostrils flared at the thought. "Aye, lass. That sounds... nice."

He was rewarded with another one of her smiles as she crossed the room toward him. It wasn't until she reached the chair that he had an inkling of what she might do, and as she moved the stack of clean cloths to the floor, he had a moment's regret that he hadn't thought to grab one to cover his nudity.

On the other hand, they *were* married. He *had* bedded her, even if she hadn't enjoyed it. And God knew she'd seen enough of him during his torment as he fought to overcome his dependence on ale. Seeing him in the bath surely wasn't enough to frighten her away.

Still, he sunk a bit lower in the water as she moved the chair behind him and reached for the soap.

But when her fingers brushed against the top of his head, he jerked away from her. "What are ye doing?"

"Washing yer hair," she responded matter-of-factly. "'Tis filthy, and I havenae been able to clean it."

"I dinnae…"

He wasn't sure what he was going to say, but when he trailed off, she hummed quietly.

"I ken, Jaimie. Ye dinnae like to be touched. So ye say." Her fingertips came to rest on his shoulder, as if urging him to relax once more. "I promise, it willnae hurt. I willnae hurt ye."

"Ye couldnae possibly," he growled, but allowed himself to be pulled back. It was easier than trying to explain the truth.

I dinnae like to be touched because it reminds me of what I've lost.

He desperately *needed* to be touched, but it so rarely happened anymore. That any mere brush was torture. This woman, this *wife* of his, had touched him more in the last weeks than anyone had in years.

And tonight was no different.

She lathered up her hands. As she dug her strong fingers into his scalp, Jaimie couldn't fight the groan of pleasure that rose in his throat. Instead, he exhaled in surrender and rested his head near her.

It was a moment before he realized his new wife was humming as she massaged his head, a peaceful little tune. The way she kneaded his scalp caused the remaining tension to drain from his shoulders and back. The heat, the cool breeze, the aftermath of his release, the song, and her touch… they all combined to relax him in a way he hadn't felt in many, many years.

Probably since before he'd met Aileen.

She raked the soap through his hair again and again, cupping her hands to pour water across individual strands, before moving, satisfied, to the next section. He knew he should just cut the whole mess off, but he'd never been able to stomach the thought. For years now, his hair had hidden the wreck of his face.

The wreck which was now exposed to his wife.

The realization came a moment before her fingertips brushed against the ruined skin of his face.

He was too peaceful to do aught more than flinch, but he did open his eyes to find her staring down at him.

"What happened?" she asked gently.

His brow twitched skeptically. "Ye haven't asked Jean already?"

Her smile was gentle as she turned her attention back to his hair. "When I lived here with—with David, he only ever spoke of ye as a courtier at the King's court. When I met ye, I didnae think it right to hear the story from anyone else."

Really? He felt his lips pull down in consideration. She hadn't relished the chance to gossip about him the way Aileen had?

He closed his eyes on a sigh and accepted the truth. This new wife of his was nothing like Aileen. Nothing like the wife he'd once wanted.

The wife David had claimed.

"'Tis no great secret," he finally said. "It happened here, so anyone could tell ye."

Her fingers were gentle now as they worked in his hair. "I dinnae want *anyone* to tell me, Jaimie."

This woman had shown him such kindness, such acceptance. Was it any wonder he loved the way she said his name?

He licked his lower lip again. "'Tis winter burn. Frost-bite, I've heard it called. I was visiting for Yuletide celebrations when Callan was five years old, and I left—I left the keep at night without a cloak." Swallowing, he refused to say her name. "When they found us—*me*, David didn't think I'd live."

With a bitter laugh, he held up his ruined hands, opening his eyes to stare at them in hatred. "I lost the tips of my fingers and..." He raked one set of ruined fingers down his cheek. "And the skin here. Aunt Jean refused to let me die, although when I realized what I'd lost, I wished she had."

He'd deserved to die, after what he'd done. What he'd *failed* to do.

Agata didn't respond to that claim, but hummed again. It was a long time before she spoke again.

"'Tis why ye drowned yerself in drink, aye? No' because of this..." She paused in her motions to gently brush against his cheek once more. "But because ye felt ye deserved it."

Stunned, Jaimie shot forward and twisted in the tub to stare at her. How had she known that?

Agata sat demurely, the Mackenzie plaid across her breast marked with water. But when she smiled, Jaimie knew she was right. And knew she knew it, too.

With a muttered curse, he turned forward once more and dunked his head under the water, digging his own ruined fingers into his hair to rinse out the soap. Maybe if he stayed under, with the muffled sounds and pressure building against his skin, he could block out her words.

I drank because I survived.

Aye, she was right.

Finally, when he couldn't hold his breath any longer and he knew the soap was rinsed out, he pulled his head upright once more, wincing at the way the long strands slapped against his skin.

"I need a drink," he muttered.

And just as the hundred other times in the last weeks, Agata was there beside him in a moment, holding out a cup of cold water.

He glared at the cup, then at her, while she smiled in encouragement. With another curse, he grabbed the cup and downed its contents.

It wasn't what he wanted, but it tasted better than he'd expected.

When he lowered the cup, she nodded and handed him a drying cloth, then crossed to the pitcher with the cup.

Still scowling, Jaimie stepped out of the tub onto the sweet-smelling rushes and began to dry himself. When he was finished, he pushed his clean, damp hair back over his shoulder and wrapped the cloth around his waist. He was holding it in place when he turned to find Agata staring at him.

Her eyes were wide, her lips slightly parted, and even from there, he could see her breasts rising and falling faster than usual. He glanced down at himself, wondering if there was a scar he'd somehow forgotten to cover, but no. She wasn't staring at his cheek or his hands. She was staring at his *chest*.

As he watched, she swallowed and took a step closer, and the realization slammed into him, she wasn't staring at him in horror or pity, but *pleasure*. She *liked* what she was looking at.

He found himself standing straighter, prouder... and was awed by his reaction to her stare. It'd been years since he'd felt this way.

"Ye're..." She cleared her throat and raised her eyes to his.

"Ye're looking better, husband. I'm glad fer Cook's pottage and bread." She stepped closer. "'Tis filled ye out."

She was right. In the last weeks, he'd been eating better—and drinking less—and it was beginning to show. His muscles ached from disuse, but he'd vowed to begin training with his brother's men once more.

But 'twould be a shame to give the cook all the credit. "Nay, lass," he forced past a dry throat. "'Tis thanks to ye, no' Cook. Ye're the one who helped me fight."

Did it make him a weak man to admit he'd needed his wife's help? His wife, who was always so sure and in control? Then mayhap he *was* a weak man.

And mayhap that didn't matter.

She blushed becomingly, but didn't drop her gaze. "I did naught but encourage ye."

"And harangue me. And nag me into eating." With a slight grin, he closed the distance between them. "And refuse to let me die, even when I begged ye to."

"Jaimie," she whispered, a note of yearning in her voice as she held up her hand… and hesitated just as her fingers would have brushed against his chest.

He swallowed, knowing what she wanted. Knowing what *he* wanted. Could he give it to her? To them both?

He could do this. He could accept her touch.

"Aye, lass?" he all but croaked as he raised his hand and pressed his palm to hers.

He watched her shudder slightly as she laced her fingers through his, and felt like matching it. His fingers were ruined, aye, but he'd long ago regained feeling in the skin covering the tips. And now he could feel her warmth and *life* under his touch, as well as see the flutter of the pulse at the base of her throat.

What would she taste like there?

They stood there a long moment, neither moving, her

hand in his, as they both concentrated on just *breathing*. After their disaster of a wedding night, when he'd taken her without seeing to her pleasure, and after the necessities of the last weeks, this was their most intimate touch.

Just holding her hand.

He closed his eyes on the sensation, knowing that despite the lovers he'd had in the past, despite what he thought he'd missed, *this* was the touch he'd been yearning for.

And that knowledge sent him pulling away, unsure if he should've forced his touch upon her again. She resisted momentarily before letting him go and running her hand across her honey-blonde braid with a nervous smile.

"I'll let ye prepare for bed, Jaimie."

"Nay." The denial slipped out before he could stop it, and he shook his head ruefully. "I mean, this is David's chamber, and I've been here long enough." He cleared his throat and looked toward the bed he'd been in more often than not over the last days. "I'll return to my own room."

When she frowned in confusion, Jaimie was struck by how sweet her lips looked.

"But this is the laird's chambers."

"Aye, and Callan will be the laird. I'm just his regent."

She glanced toward the door to her chambers, and seemed to come to some decision. Straightening her shoulders, she offered him a small nod. "Truthfully, I kenned yer brother less than a year, and I didnae care for this room either. 'Tis too… hard."

She understood.

He felt the right side of his mouth—the undamaged side—pull up in a wry grin, or as close as he could manage these days. "Aye."

Still, he made no move to exit the chamber, to cross the hall to the room which had been his since birth. And maybe that was the sign she'd been waiting for, because suddenly, she darted forward again and took his hand.

But this time, instead of standing there holding him, she tugged him through the door to her chambers. He followed, holding the cloth around his waist with his free hand, for there was naught else to do.

Once in her smaller room—the room she'd occupied when she'd been his brother's wife, the room where he'd taken her on their wedding night—she took a deep breath and seemed to be in control once more.

"Are ye hungry? I can have supper sent up."

Not sure what her plan was, Jaimie just shook his head. "Ye're all feeding me more'n I can stand. I'm still full from the chicken pottage." Although it *had* been good, and he'd had a second helping for the first time in… well, it'd been a long time since he'd cared enough about aught besides ale to reach for a second serving.

Nodding, she murmured, "Good," as she tugged him toward the bed.

And right then and there, Jaimie decided he didn't mind his wife taking control.

She pulled back the covers and nudged him down onto the mattress, then turned away. She stepped behind the screen to do whatever she needed, and Jaimie tugged the cloth from around his hips. He tossed it toward a nearby chair and swung his bare feet—and his bare arse—into her bed.

As he pulled the linen up around his waist, he realized he was already semi-erect. It was hard to imagine being able to spill again so soon, but if that's what his strong, in-control wife wanted, he'd give it to her as best as he could.

Wouldn't he?

He listened to her moving behind the screen, and swallowed thickly. What he'd done to her on their wedding night, that hadn't been what was proper between a husband and wife. He'd been angry, and more than a little drunk, and had treated her like a whore.

And she'd treated him like a husband.

Swallowing a groan, he closed his eyes and leaned back against the pillow, shame for his actions flowing through his veins. Aye, what he'd done had been wrong, and if she ever showed any interest in having him bed her again, he'd do it properly.

But it would be her choice. He'd wait until he knew what *she* wanted.

When the bed dipped, he knew she'd slid in beside him. Steeling his heart—and reminding his cock to behave—Jaimie opened his eyes. With the shutters still open, there was just enough of the fading light to see her lying beside him, staring at the ceiling.

Taking a deep breath, he rolled over on his side to face her. This position meant his good cheek was pressed into the pillow, and with his dark hair spread out behind him, he felt on display to his wife.

This is who I am. Half man, half monster, weak and incapable of leading.

Let her decide if she still wanted him.

In one movement, Agata rolled over as well, mirroring his pose. His hands itched to reach for her, to pull her closer. But he laid there, holding his breath and wondering why she'd led him to her bed.

With a small smile, she reached up and placed her hand to his ruined cheek, the one on full view now. When he didn't flinch away, she pressed her palm against his skin, and inhaled deeply.

And damn him, but he did as well, reveling in her sweet scent.

Reveling in the sensation of being here in her bed with *her*.

The hot bath and the earlier release had taken their toll on him. So, too, the days of fighting the drink, of the fever as his strong wife helped him to victory. As the heartbeats ticked by, Jaimie felt his eyelids sinking.

He blinked them open once, to see her fighting exhaustion as well. The realization made him smile, as much as he could. When she saw that, her answering smile was sweet.

And as his eyes closed again, he knew that no bedding would feel better than lying here while his wife, who'd fought for him, touched him so gently.

He remembered what she'd said that day after their wedding. They'd been speaking of the hold the drink had over him, and she'd said he must find something to replace it in his heart. When he'd asked what, she'd said, "Mayhap his new wife."

As sleep claimed him, Jaimie realized she was right. For the first time in years, he didn't want a drink. But his whole body yearned for the woman lying beside him.

His whole body… and—he was beginning to suspect—his whole heart.

CHAPTER 6

AGATA'S EYES flew open with a gasp she only just managed to muffle. There was a large, warm body behind her, and she froze, hoping she hadn't woken him. When a long moment went by, and Jaimie's breathing remained even, she slowly relaxed again into his hold.

One of his arms was around her, his hand pressing against her belly and tucking her into the curve of his pelvis. It felt… right. This was the first time she'd ever woken in a man's arms, and she couldn't deny how comforting it was.

And as his warm breath stirred the hairs on the back of her neck, Agata slowly smiled.

Goodness, this certainly was different from sharing a bed with her sisters, wasn't it?

Word had arrived from home with news of Pearl's safe return—exactly as Citrine predicted—and marriage to the Sinclair Hound… again, exactly as Citrine predicted. Agata had written back to update her sisters on her search for hints on the location of the jewels—futile, at this point—her husband's progress, and how proud she was of him.

Aye, she couldn't be more pleased with the changes in her

husband in the last two weeks. The man she'd married had been only half-there, really; the drink had controlled his actions and thoughts. While she knew Jaimie was still hurting over whatever had turned him to spirits all those years ago, at least he was fully here with her. Now that he was no longer reliant on ale to dull the pain, she could help him heal from that suffering.

Of course, I have nae idea how to do that.

Behind her, Jaimie made a noise between a mumble and a sigh. His arm tightened around her, pulling her rear end more snugly against his *member*. Her eyes widened as she felt it nestle against her, just slightly harder than it had been a moment before.

The knowledge left her with a strange sort of ache in the center of her body.

In the weeks since their wedding, she'd thought of the way Jaimie had bedded her. It had been cold, aye, but not controlled. When he'd entered her, she could sense his barely contained emotions and reactions, and had marveled at their power. What would their mating be like once he allowed himself to let go, to fully *feel*?

Experimentally, she shifted against him. When she felt the length of him grow against her backside, her lips curved up in a small, triumphant smile. *She* did that. Her husband might try to hide his feelings—why?—but here and now, she could influence him.

Curious now, she slowly moved her hand toward his, where it rested right below her breasts. Remembering the way it had felt last night to twine her fingers through his, she wondered *why* he'd been so adamant about not liking to be touched. After the time spent washing his hair and holding his hand, and waking up pressed against him like this... it was clear he didn't mind being touched all *that* much.

So, she brushed her fingertips across the back of his hand,

and when he made no sound of objection, did it again. Then, gently, she rested her hand against his. His hand would be much larger than hers, but with a third of his fingers missing, they were of a similar length.

What had sent him out into the cold all those years ago? Had it been worth it, to lose a part of himself like this? She suspected, not for the first time, that some fingertips hadn't been all he'd lost that day.

And how had he learned to adapt in the years since? In the time she'd known him, she hadn't seen Jaimie do much with his hands. Even the food he'd eaten had been simple to hold. He said he rode—and that she could accompany him!—so he must be able to hold the reins. Could he hold a stylus? Wield a sword? A paint brush?

On their wedding night, these hands had stroked himself, then prepared her for his entry. What would they feel like on her breasts? On her hips?

On her... *there?*

She realized she'd tightened her hold on his hand as her breathing had gotten shallower. The thought of him caressing her, of bedding her again... it made her skin feel all tingly. She squirmed against him again, and was gratified to feel him exhale and mumble against the back of her neck as his member hardened further.

He was naked. She was wearing only her shift. He was *obviously* interested in her as a woman, and judging from the ache between her legs, Agata was ready to explore her physical relationship with her husband.

But just like last night, she held herself back, stopped herself from rolling over and demanding he bed her again.

Aye, it may have worked on their wedding night, when her future hung in the balance and she desperately needed to be accepted as Lady Mackenzie. But now...? Now, she knew she had to tread gently and allow *him* to make the decision to bed her. Whatever his issues with *touch* and allowing himself to feel, she knew they were tied with his longtime dependence on the drink.

He was changing, this husband of hers, and although she was used to being in control, she needed to wait and have faith that he was changing for the better. All she could do was continue to stand beside him and help, and pray he'd eventually want to reach for her in the night.

Of course, there was nothing to say she couldn't hurry things along.

With another small smile, she wriggled her rear end against him again. At the same time, she gently coaxed his hand higher, until the edges of his fingers brushed against the bottom swell of her breast. When she shifted yet again, she was rewarded with a small groan.

The hitch in his breathing told her he was waking up, and when he tightened his hold and pulled her firmly against him, she felt like gloating. He was awake, and he was touching her!

He hummed, a sleepy, satisfied sort of sound which made her smile.

"Lass, ye're causing all sorts of—"

She was already halfway turned in his arms, delighted to discover whatever it was she was causing, when the door to her chamber burst open.

"Aunt Agata! Aunt Agata! I found another one!"

She swallowed down her sigh of disappointment, but beside her, Jaimie wasn't so restrained. He rolled onto his back and threw his forearm across his eyes with a heartfelt groan. She wasn't sure if he was more irritated at the early-morning visit or being interrupted as things were being *caused*. But either way, she was smiling as she turned to the boy.

Usually, Callan had no compulsions against throwing himself onto her bed and bouncing until she woke fully, today he skidded to a stop when he saw she wasn't alone. His wide-eyed gaze snapped to Jaimie, and his mouth dropped open.

"Uncle Jaimie! What are ye doing here?"

"*Nothing,*" the man mumbled from under his arm, and he sounded so disgruntled that Agata's smile grew.

Determined to foster a sense of normalcy in the boy, Agata sat up nonchalantly, tugging her shift into place. "Jaimie and I are married, Callan," she reminded him in a gentle voice. "'Tis no' uncommon for a husband to spend the night with his wife."

The boy narrowed his eyes suspiciously. "Father never spent the night with ye."

And she'd never wanted him to. She nodded. "Yer Uncle Jaimie isnae yer father."

That seemed to satisfy the boy. Callan shrugged and climbed up on the bed. He threw himself across her legs and cradled his chin in his hands. "He doesnae look sick anymore," he critiqued thoughtfully, kicking his heels.

"I think he's feeling better." Then she whispered conspiratorially, "He said we might go riding together today."

"What?" The lad jerked upright. "Even me? He said that?"

"I'm *right here,*" Jaimie growled. "Stop talking about me as if I'm a pile of bedding."

Agata pressed her lips together to hide her smile as Callan rolled in between the adults and loomed over Jaimie.

"Can I go with ye, Uncle Jaimie? Please?"

It warmed her heart to see how the lad had taken his uncle's instructions to heart. Almost immediately following their talk, Callan had started referring to his relatives much less formally. His father's legacy was slowly being erased, and she was thrilled to be helping. Now this precious stepson of hers—or was he now her nephew?—felt fully comfortable bouncing on her bed with an eager expression.

Just in case Jaimie didn't understand the significance of the boy's actions, she nudged her husband's shin, which was still sprawled near hers. He grunted in response and moved his forearm just enough to peer up at his nephew.

"Has yer riding improved aught?" he asked.

Callan frowned. "I didnae *fall* that time, and ye ken it! I was *jumping*."

"Fair enough." As Jaimie sighed and removed his arm completely from his face, the covers fell enough to reveal his chest. "Ye can catch *me* if I fall off."

The lad giggled and poked his uncle in the shoulder. "I remember ye're a good rider, Uncle Jaimie. Ye used to let me sit in front of ye when ye'd come home from court to visit. Father said it was a waste of time, but I remember Mother laughing."

Her husband's gaze darted away from the boy's and fixed on the ceiling… but Agata could tell he wasn't seeing it.

"Aye, she laughed whenever I spent time with ye," he finally said in a rough whisper. "But that was a long time ago."

Before his injury? Certainly before his dependency on ale. What else had happened in that time? And why did he close up whenever David's first wife was mentioned?

She tugged on Callan's leg to make him back up. "Why did ye burst in on us this morning, ye wee hellion?"

"*Oh!*" His face lit up with excitement once more. "I forgot to tell ye! I found another one!" He took a deep breath. "I havenae gone in, because I thought we could explore it together."

"Found *what*, Callan?"

He bounced again. "Another passageway! We've explored all the ones I kenned about, aye? But since this is a new one to me—to us—the clue might be there!"

She grabbed the boy's hand in her excitement. "Aye!" She whispered breathlessly. "The jewels! We might—"

"What's this?" Jaimie growled, sitting up.

The sheet fell around his waist, and Agata was distracted by the sight of his chest. Just as last night, her fingers itched to touch all that skin, to see if the small dark hairs which peppered it were as soft as they looked. She wanted to press her palm against his heart and feel it beating, and her throat went dry at the thought.

"Agata?" he prompted her impatiently.

"The..." She had to lick her lips to continue, and forced her gaze back up to his face. She'd never hated a promise more than at that moment, knowing she had to hide her sisters' grand hunt from her husband. She couldn't lie to him! "Callan... has been giving me a tour of the keep's secret passageways, husband."

"They're *secret* for a reason, ye ken," he growled again, turning his glare on the boy. "Ye're no' to go in them alone. Some are dangerous. They're only to be used in an emergency, and if everyone kens about them, they willnae be secret."

Callan lifted his chin. "They're no' dangerous."

"No' the ones *ye've* been in. But they're no' maintained, and the floor is unsteady in some. The boards have given way— well, it doesnae matter."

"How do *ye* ken?"

Agata tensed at the stubborn challenge in the lad's voice, wondering how Jaimie would handle it. The way David might have? Or would he shut himself off again?

He did neither. Instead, her husband sighed and scrubbed a hand across his face, ending with a yawn as he scratched at the sparse beard he'd grown in an attempt to cover his scar.

"I *ken*, lad, because I grew up here, remember?"

Callan's eyes brightened. "Ye mean *ye* explored the passageways, too? Do ye ken of any more—"

"It matters naught, does it? Because ye'll cease yer explorations at once."

His glare was fierce, but when the boy giggled, it was clear Callan had seen through the attempt at discipline.

"What if I'm with ye? Or with Aunt Agata? Can we explore then?"

Jaimie just rolled his eyes. "Yer aunt is a smart woman, and I trust her to ken what's dangerous. And now…"

When he swung his legs off the bed and stood up, Callan giggled at the sight of his uncle's naked buttocks. Agata's eyes went round, and she completely forgot to be flattered by Jaimie's compliment.

As the man reached for the drying cloth he'd used the night before, she remembered the heat she'd felt earlier in his arms. Her husband's lithe form tapered to a fine set of cheeks, and she wouldn't mind looking at them a bit longer. She was disappointed when he wrapped the cloth around himself and turned with a mock glare as he scratched at his jaw once more.

"And now, I'm going to shave this mess off, afore our ride."

He stomped out of the room, and Agata's gaze followed him. *Shave?* And he was *teasing* them? Aye, her husband was feeling much improved, that was obvious.

And what was even better, she *liked* who he was becoming.

"UNCLE JAIMIE! WATCH THIS!"

The lad kicked his pony and went tearing off across the meadow, whooping war cries like a real warrior. Jaimie found himself holding his breath as Callan's animal cleared a small stream, and he had to admit the lad rode well.

Beside him, his wife chuckled, a surprisingly sensual sound. "He's been so proud of himself. I'm glad ye could see him."

Jaimie's fist tightened around the reins. When was the last

time he'd gone riding? Since returning to Mackenzie lands, surely, but he couldn't remember a specific time.

The drink had done that to him. Even now, he thirsted, but forced his attention away from the niggling need and focused on the woman beside him.

"He has reason to be proud. He rides like a Mackenzie, and deserves a real mount soon."

"Oh, aye." She flashed him a smile. "But ye'll be hard-pressed to woo him away from Thunder. That's what he calls the pony."

Thunder. A fanciful name for the wee beast. Jaimie found himself smiling as he clucked his own horse into motion.

As the two of them rode along the valley, he kept an eye on his nephew in the distance. The lad had turned his pony around and was picking his way back at a more leisurely pace. That allowed Jaimie some privacy...

He glanced at Agata to see her frowning down at her horse's right leg. What was wrong?

"Agata?"

When she looked up, her smile flashed brightly, and he assumed that meant the horse was fine.

"Aye, Jaimie?"

The way she smiled like that, the way she said his name... it made Jaimie forget himself for a moment. He wanted it to be real *so badly*, but with every breath he took, he expected reality to come crashing back and remind him he couldn't call such a beautiful, strong woman *his*.

He cleared his throat. "The jewels?"

Her brows dipped in. "What about us?"

Us? Oh, aye. He remembered Aunt Jean explaining that the Sinclair's four daughters were known as the Sinclair Jewels. Agata herself had been named for the agate found along the rocky beaches. Is that what she'd meant...?

"This morning, Callan said the two of ye would explore the secret passageways for clues to 'the jewels'—dinnae deny it."

"Deny it?" Agata pulled her horse to a stop and shook her head. "Why would I deny it?"

Without waiting for an answer, she swung down from the saddle, and Jaimie was momentarily distracted by the sight of a shapely calf before her skirts settled back around her boots. She murmured to the horse as she ducked under his neck and picked up its foreleg.

"Because those passageways—what *are* ye doing?"

"There's a hitch in his gait. I dinnae think he's injured, but—"

In an instant, he'd swung down and was bent beside her. Jaimie hummed in agreement as they examined the hoof together. "Mayhap a bruise? Best to walk him."

He reached for the animal's reins and turned both horses toward the distant keep. She could ride with Callan or... Jaimie swallowed suddenly. Or with *him*.

Before he could broach the subject of the jewels and clues and passageways again, Callan raced up on Thunder, kicking up pebbles as he reined the pony to a halt and jumped down.

"Did ye see me, Uncle Jaimie? Did ye see us take that creek? Are we walking now? Why are we walking? Aunt Agata, did ye see how fast we were going?"

She seemed used to the boy's energy, because she just nodded serenely. "Ye were fast as lightening, Callan."

"That's why his name's Thunder, ye ken. Why are ye standing around?"

"My horse is limping, and I dinnae want to lame him. Yer uncle and I were waiting for ye."

"Uncle Jaimie!" Wide-eyed, the boy turned back to him. "Did ye see us jump?"

Feeling a little frantic at being the center of attention,

Jaimie did his best to follow Agata's example. "A—aye. Ye'll be a braw hunter one day."

"I ken!" the boy gasped. "Ye should've seen it, Uncle!" He scrambled up on a boulder and took imaginary aim down an arrow shaft. "Thunder nigh *squashed* a pair of rabbits! They took off running like their tails were afire! If I'd had my bow —!" He let loose the imaginary arrow with a satisfied "Thwack!"

Agata gave an exaggerated shudder. "I dislike rabbit. Could ye hunt down a sheep for me? I prefer mutton."

"*Mutton?*" the boy groaned. He rolled his eyes toward his uncle in camaraderie. "Hunting *mutton!* Uncle, ye need to take me out hunting for stag. That'll show her what a real man can do, aye?"

Even as Callan slapped his chest with an open palm, Jaimie hid his wince. *A real man?* The lad hadn't meant insult, but…

"Sorry, nephew." Unbidden, Jaimie's ruined hand curled into a fist by his thigh. "I cannot hunt anymore."

The boy froze and cocked his head, studying Jaimie. "Why no'?"

Resisting the urge to glance at Agata, to see the pity in her eyes, Jaimie swallowed and lifted his right hand. He tucked the reins against his palm with his thumb, and held up his stunted fingers.

"I cannae draw a bowstring."

To his surprise, the boy flicked his own fingers dismissively and rolled his eyes. "Yer fingers still bend. Ye can draw a bow," he said matter-of-factly as he slid down the boulder. "If ye can wield a sword, ye can draw a bow."

Jaimie wanted to snap at the boy, to ask him when *he'd* become an expert. But at the same time, he hesitated. *Could* he wield a bow anymore? The same as riding a horse, he couldn't remember the last time he'd tried.

Callan had sensed his hesitation, because the boy

approached with a solemn nod. "If ye need help, Uncle, I'd be happy to practice with ye."

Beside him, Agata made a noise which might have been a sniff of laughter, but Jaimie didn't dare turn to confirm it. Instead, he raised his brow at his nephew.

"And ye think I can just re-grow fingers?"

"Nay, but I ken ye can do aught ye put yer mind to. That's what Aunt Agata taught me."

This time, Jaimie's gaze slid to her, but her wide brown eyes were innocent.

"Ye *did* call me a smart woman just this morning, husband."

He had, hadn't he?

Callan clasped his hands behind his back and strolled back toward his pony, giving a good impression of old Edward, the seneschal. "Aunt Agata taught me to paint when I was just a wee lad, ye ken."

"Ye're *still* a wee lad," Jaimie growled.

The boy whirled to glare at his uncle. "*Wee'r* than I am now." He frowned as he composed himself, while Jaimie tried not to chuckle. "But if she could teach me to paint when I was just…"

He began to count on his fingers, obviously trying to remember how old he'd been when David had married Agata.

"Five," Jaimie helpfully supplied.

"Almost six!" Callan corrected, then shrugged. "If I could learn to paint then, ye can learn, too."

Where the hell had this conversation gotten to? "Learn to paint?" Jaimie asked in confusion.

"Aye!"

He rolled his eyes. "Why would I want to learn to paint?"

"Because," Agata jumped in with a quiet surety, "'tis an excellent way to show yer nephew ye see value in the things he values."

Jaimie's mouth snapped shut.

She was right. He'd gone through hell for the last few weeks just to ensure Callan would be raised by a man who understood him, and believed he should be allowed to express himself. Showing an interest in something like painting, which Callan valued, would prove to the boy his talents were appreciated.

And he could spend time with his intriguing wife, as well.

Unbidden, his gaze dropped to his hand. Could he learn to paint? Could he do half the things he'd thought part of his past?

And if he could, did that still make him the failure he'd long thought?

Her hand closed around his, and he felt that now-familiar warmth spread up his arm, especially when he met her eyes and saw her smile.

"I'd be happy to teach ye, husband," she said quietly.

Without waiting for his response, Callan whooped with joy and threw himself atop his pony. "Ye'll be mixing paints in no time, Uncle!" he yelled in encouragement, just before he jabbed his heels into the animal's sides and they set off like a shot toward home.

Jaimie couldn't help the way his lips twitched at the boy's enthusiasm. When he glanced at Agata, he discovered she was gazing at him with pride.

Reluctantly, he pulled his hand away and nodded toward her horse. "We had better start back as well, and have the stablemaster look at his hoof."

She glanced toward the horse, and he took the opportunity to step closer and close his hands around her middle. It was somehow easier to manage without her staring so intently at him, but he lifted her into his saddle with only a slight pull at long-unused muscles. And he could admit he liked the way she gasped in surprise and clamped down on his shoulders.

Still, he hid his grin as he swung up into the saddle behind her, and settled her atop his thighs. Pretending nonchalance he didn't quite feel, he nudged his horse into a walk and tugged at her animal's reins until he was content the mare would follow.

She said nothing, but sat stiffly in his lap. Jaimie found himself praying he hadn't overstepped, hadn't angered her. Since they'd woken this morning, he'd wanted to have her in his arms again, and a lame horse was as good an excuse as he could hope for. But now that she was here, did she think he'd gone too far? Was she disgusted at the thought of being held by a man like him?

Yer treasure's in the south-land. Aunt Jean had said that whenever Jaimie had gone off adventuring, and even in the months since he'd returned. But more and more, he was beginning to suspect his aunt was wrong.

His treasure was right here, sitting on his lap.

After what seemed like an eternity, he watched the tension in her shoulders ease, watched her take a breath. Slowly, she allowed herself to slump backward, to press her back against his chest. He easily took her weight, glad for the chance to support *her* for a change.

She made a contented noise in her throat and tucked her head against his shoulder. He placed the mare's reins under one of his thighs, and reached around to grasp his own reins with both hands, which meant his arms were once more around his wife.

Where they belonged.

CHAPTER 7

BY THE FOURTH time Jaimie read through the trading contract, the words were beginning to blur. He sighed and scrubbed his hand over his face, feeling a proud sort of weariness. Two months ago—*a month ago*—before his marriage, the words would've blurred because *everything* was blurry, thanks to the drink. But today, it was because he'd read and re-read read the damn thing so many times he probably had it memorized.

Of course, he still needed a drink.

With another sigh, he reached for the tankard Edward kept full of cool water, and although it wasn't exactly what he was craving, it eased his thirst. He plunked it back down atop the carved map which stood in the center of the desk.

"Is everything acceptable, milord?" the seneschal asked from his chair on the other side of the desk.

Jaimie nodded wearily at the old man. They'd begun to work like this recently, each focused on their own tasks, but near enough that Edward could answer any questions he had. And it was embarrassing to admit he *did* have questions.

Apparently in the last few years, the seneschal had been the only one standing between the Mackenzies and ruin.

While Jaimie had been drinking himself into oblivion, and Callan off training and being a child, the old man had done his best to keep the alliances strong and the clan safe and well-fed.

It was galling to realize not only how useless he'd been, but how much he owed his seneschal.

"Aye, Edward. We'll send the wool down to Inverness, then from there to Leith and eventually France. Ye're right about the prices we'll get, but we'll have to bear the cost of the trip in mind."

And damn if the old man didn't look *proud* as he scrambled to get the sealing wax prepared. "Ye've made the right decision, Jaimie," he said fondly.

Jaimie's throat was dry when he reached for the little dipper of hot wax, and he didn't think it had anything to do with ale. Nay, it was emotion which caused him to swallow so thickly. He'd been useless for so long, believing himself to be half a man—a man with no honor, no purpose beyond the next cup of ale.

But now? Well, now he was still struggling to learn what needed to be done as the Mackenzie regent, but he was *proud* of what little he'd managed to accomplish in the short amount of time.

And he realized pride was important.

When the wax was ready, he pulled his father's signet ring from his thumb—the only finger which could still hold the thing—and pressed it into the wax. One day he'd tie it on a leather thong and hang it from Callan's neck until the lad was big enough to wear it the way David had. But for now, Jaimie would do the best he could with it.

When the door opened, he'd half expected it to be a serving wench with another ewer of water, on behalf of his wife. It seemed Agata and Edward were involved in some kind of conspiracy—with Aunt Jean presiding—to drown him. And as much as he wanted a sip of spirits, he couldn't be irritated with them.

Besides, he was coming to learn there were *other* things a man could crave just as much. Such as the taste of his wife's lips.

Which is probably why, when Agata was the one who stepped through the door, his exhaustion fell away in the blink of an eye. All of his senses were focused on her and the way she smiled when she met his eyes.

His cock jumped to attention under his kilt.

Still, when he realized her arms were full, he shifted discreetly as he stood and came around the desk to help her.

Edward cleared his throat and gathered up the scrolls and parchments they'd been working on. There was a twinkle in the old man's eye when he nodded to both of them. "I'll ensure the messenger gets this directly, milord. I'll leave ye two to…" He cleared his throat, nodded again, and hurried out the door.

No doubt to report straight to Aunt Jean, the old bastard.

And if Jaimie was being honest, he had to admit that Aunt Jean had been brilliant when she'd made the marriage contract with Duncan Sinclair. Just look what miracles Agata had wrought in a short amount of time!

As he reached her, Agata's smile turned grateful and she lifted her elbow to allow him to remove the odd-looking frame she was carrying under her arm. He held the bundle of planks at arm's length and peered at them thoughtfully.

"What is this?"

"'Tis an easel," she called laughingly over her shoulder. "Bring it over here so I can show ye how to set it up!"

That's when he realized she was carrying a board under her other arm, and a collection of pots and vials on a tray.

"Is this the painting ye threatened me with, lass?"

"It wasnae a threat, husband, but a promise. Callan has been pleading to paint with ye since our ride." As she spoke, she deftly assembled the easel and placed the board on it. "I put him off, explaining ye have important work to do, but I'm no' sure how much longer he'll last afore he explodes."

Satisfied, she turned and grinned at Jaimie. "And I thought ye might like yer first lesson to be in private, afore ye allow a seven-year-old to humiliate ye."

He rolled his eyes as he crossed to her, instinct telling him to place his hands on her hips, to draw her closer as he teased her. Although they were married, although she had changed his life in such a short amount of time, they hadn't reached that level of intimacy yet. He'd bedded her, aye, but not since that first night. In the last sennight, since he'd taken on the mantle of responsibility, since that ride where she'd sat on his lap, safe and content… they had not touched again. No matter how much he ached to have her in his arms, no matter that the night he'd spent sleeping beside her had been his best sleep he could remember, he knew the next step had to come from her.

And so, he halted just out of arm's reach. Because he knew if he was any closer, he'd be hard-pressed to stop touching her. "And so ye thought to interrupt me in the middle of my important work, wife?" he asked with a fierce scowl. "I'm Callan's regent! That means my sorry arse has work to do, ye ken!"

And damn him if he didn't catch a seductive glint in her eyes as the corners of her lips pulled up. "Aye," she breathed, "but I ken a hard-working man needs to take breaks sometimes, and this seemed as good a time as any."

Vaguely, Jaimie realized he was alone in the solar with his wife. This room had always been David's, but in the last sennight, Jaimie had made it his. And now, with Agata here, he suddenly wanted to make it *theirs*.

As if she could read his mind, Agata stepped toward him. "I want…"

He found himself leaning toward her, straining, *aching.* "Aye, lass?" he asked breathlessly.

Suddenly, she flushed and dropped her gaze to his chin. Was she nervous? "I want ye to ken how proud I am of ye. And the work ye've done. If ye really dinnae want an interruption, I can leave ye alone…"

Jaimie's breath whooshed out of him on a desperate little laugh. "Believe me, lass, the last thing I want ye to do right now is leave."

She peeked up at him, and Jaimie was entranced with this side of his take-charge wife. He tried a grin in response, and was gratified when her eyes flashed in pleasure. His gaze dropped to her lips, and the way they parted in surprise. He dragged his tongue over his lower lip, wondering yet again how hers would taste.

He'd nigh forgotten what he'd blurted, when she shyly asked, "And the verra first thing ye want me to do right now?"

Mayhap it would have been smarter to think through his response, but Jaimie quickly replied, "Trust me, lass, ye dinnae need to ken what's going on in my mind when I look at ye."

"Why not?" she challenged.

There was the feisty wife he was falling in love with. He raised his brow.

"I mean," she clarified, "why do ye think I dinnae want to ken?"

That question hadn't been what he'd expected. Flustered, Jaimie ran one hand through his hair, pulling it away from his face before he realized what he'd done. Knowing how close he stood to her, and how all of his scars were on display, he quickly dropped the locks over his left cheek.

"Because what a man thinks about when he sees a woman, especially a woman as desirable as ye, isnae fit conversation."

Apparently not understanding his warning, she took yet another step closer until mere inches separated them. She tilted her head back and met his eyes. "Surely ye dinnae believe that? Surely 'tis acceptable for a wife to ken what her husband is feeling when he looks at her? For her to ken what he wants from her?"

And that's when she reached up and, as if it was the most natural thing in the world, tucked his hair behind his ear once more.

Aye, it would have been smart to step away then. But the shock of her touch burned him, burned as deeply as the cold had that winter night when he'd gone looking for Aileen. Aileen, who'd once touched him so gently, but as he'd soon realized, never with the same compassion Agata now showed.

Aileen had made him who he was today. Not just the ruined drunk, but the man without honor.

The man who'd bedded his brother's wife.

"Jaimie?" she prompted, and he remembered she was still waiting for a response.

So he gave her as much of an explanation as he could. "I ken what ye deserve, Agata, and it isnae a husband like me."

She frowned as she dropped her hand back to her side. "Do ye think I deserve a husband like David? Big and brawny, and so certain he had the right of things, he wouldnae consider aught else? Ye think Callan and I deserve a hard man like that?"

Flustered, Jaimie *did* step away, shaking his head. "Nay, God kens I cursed that part of him plenty of times." In desperation, he held up his hands, palms out. "But ye deserve a whole man, Agata, a husband with honor who'll treat ye that way. Instead, ye're stuck with—"

Without waiting for him to finish, she grabbed his hand, twining her fingers through his, pressing their palms together.

"Ye think ye're not whole? Ye think ye're ruined?"

"Aye, I ken it!" The words burst out of him, part relieved, part incredulous she didn't see it. With a jerk of his chin, he dislodged the hair from behind his ears so it swung back in front of his scar. "I ken who I used to be, Agata, and I ken who I've become."

"Nay, Jaimie," she said gently. "That's who ye *had* become. Ye're becoming someone else now." She lifted their clasped hands a little higher. "Callan had the right of it. Yer fingers bend, so ye can draw a bow. Ye can still wield a sword and a stylus, even if ye mostly tell Edward what to write. Those are the two most important things a laird—or a laird's regent—needs, aye?

God Almighty, but her eyes sparkled when she was passionate! This close, Jaimie could see the flecks of gold sprinkled throughout their dark depths, and was completely entranced.

"Aye," he whispered, not sure what he was agreeing to. "But they're not the only things."

Her lips lifted into a smile. "Then together, we'll learn the rest."

He couldn't seem to look away, even when he shook his head in denial. "I… lass, nay. My hands…"

As if to illustrate his point, he tightened his grip on her fingers just briefly before releasing her. But rather than remind her how broken he was, a small laugh slipped out of her lips.

"Oh, Jaimie! There's naught yer hands cannae do."

Without waiting for him to deny it, she lifted his left hand, untwined their fingers, and gripped him around the wrist. Staring into his eyes, she brought his ruined fingers to her face…and brushed them down her cheek.

The sensation of her smooth skin under his sent a shudder through him, and he had to close his eyes on the burst of desire which had nearly overwhelmed him. How long since he had allowed himself to touch a woman like this? Not taking her from behind, but from where they touched at the most intimate places... really *touched*. Caressed her.

Love her.

Over three years. That's how long it'd been. Aileen hadn't been the last, but she'd been the first. The first to show him how much pleasure could be found in *touch*.

And now, not only was Agata suffering his touch, she was encouraging it.

"See?" she whispered, her voice floating across his skin made him shudder again. "Ye feel that, do ye no'?"

"Aye," he managed to choke out.

She lifted his hand again and brushed his fingers across her face. Then, while he was still reeling from the memory of a woman's skin, she pressed his palm to her cheek and inhaled deeply.

His eyes flew open at the sound, which was so much like a noise of pleasure, he thought he was in his chambers at the royal palace once more, one—or more—of the queen's ladies wrapped in his arms. But nay, he wasn't in bed, and he wasn't naked... but it felt the same.

There was something in Agata's gaze... something hopeful and *yearning*.

"See, Jaimie?" she whispered the question. "Yer hands are quite capable. Capable of feeling. Capable of touching. Capable of giving pleasure."

And with that, she lifted his other hand and placed his palm across her heavy breast.

He rocked forward, his hand flexing in response to the long-forgotten sensation.

Knowing full well he was holding his breath, Jaimie's eyes widened—part in shock, part in fear, and partly because his cock was suddenly rock-hard.

"'Tis wonderful, husband," she whispered. Then she lowered her hand.

And for a long moment, Jaimie wasn't sure if he should lower his, too. He was torn between doing the right thing and the hunger which had settled low in his gut. Then she made the decision for him by taking a deep breath and pushing her breast into his palm.

With a groan of surrender, he dropped his hand from her check to her other breast, but refused to release her gaze. Nay, this was at *her* urging, and he wouldn't look away. Instead, he held her gaze captive while he brushed his thumbs across her nipples. They might be covered in a layer of wool and her chemise, but he could feel the small pebbles nonetheless. Her breasts were heavy, and he loved the size and feel of them.

He wanted to lower his lips to her neck, to the collar of her gown. He wanted to taste, to lick, to suckle. He squeezed her once more, and loved the way her eyes widened and her nostrils flared.

It had been a long time since he'd been with a woman who didn't take coin, but he hadn't forgotten the signs of a woman's arousal.

They'd gone about things the wrong way, hadn't they? He'd bedded her on their wedding night, cruelly and without thought to their future. But now... doing something as simple as caressing her breasts while both of them were fully clothed seemed like the biggest step forward since she'd held his hand last week.

"Ye see, Jaimie? Yer hands are *quite* capable."

And despite his vow to give her control, to let her tell him when she was ready, he was already tempted to capture her lips... then she stepped back, out of reach.

His excitement abated, as did his erection.

"Now, we have work to do."

Jaimie actually staggered as she turned to the table where she'd placed her tray and began pulling out vials. She'd released him from his trance so abruptly, he felt weak.

God Almighty, but his palms itched to hold her again. He *ached* to hold her again. But she clearly wasn't ready. She'd been teaching him a lesson, a lesson about his abilities, and it had worked.

He clenched his hands, determined to keep the memory of her perfect breasts rubbing against him, and took a deep breath.

She was the one who controlled this—whatever *this* was between them. If she wasn't prepared for him to do aught more than cup her breasts, then that would be enough for him.

She was speaking again. He took a deep breath, his hands still clenched at his side, and forced himself to focus on her words, as if his world hadn't just been shaken to its core.

"This is malachite, which I've crushed already." Carefully, she poured some of the green powder into a shallow dish, then did the same with some white powder. "And this is lead white. 'Tis created using the same method as verdigris, only in this case, it's lead—no' copper—which is suspended over a caustic liquid like vinegar, then sealed for a month. The powder which forms is scraped off and can be used to make paint."

When she glanced over at him, her expression asking if he was listening, Jaimie made himself nod. He was still reeling from her casual touch, but realized if he ever wanted to know his wife, he needed to pay attention now.

"And to make paint, ye mix the powder with egg, do ye no'?"

Her expression brightened instantly. "Aye! This is why it's called tempera. I mix it with the white part of an egg and some vinegar." She turned back to the tray and picked up a small vial. She continued to lecture as she poured some of the liquid into the dish. "Tempera paint is verra moist and requires many layers to create the correct hue. It needs a steady and patient hand."

Jaimie couldn't help his dismissive snort. "I dinnae see how ye expect me to do it, then."

She'd been right earlier, when she'd said Edward did most of the writing for matters of business for the clan. Although Jaimie had been educated as well as David, the loss of his fingers meant holding a stylus was difficult. In the days since he'd begun to take over clan affairs from the seneschal, they'd found it easier to limit Jaimie to signing his name. If he couldn't hold a stylus to do aught more than that, how did she expect him to hold a paintbrush?

Without turning, she clucked her tongue in disapproval. "One day, husband, ye'll have enough confidence to pick up a paintbrush. But today..."

When she turned, he saw she was holding the dish with the green powder. Only now, with intense concentration, she was mixing the powder into a sort of paste.

"This is a new technique, coming from Italy. The paint takes forever to dry, but by mixing it with oil instead of egg white, 'tis much thicker and more vibrant. Also..." She peeked up at him with an impish smile, "It spreads thicker and can be controlled easier. We willnae need a paintbrush."

He frowned. "I dinnae understand," he admitted.

Without explaining herself, she thrust the dish toward him and reached for the dish of lead white paint. When that was prepared to her satisfaction, she sent him another smile.

"Watch," she commanded and stepped up to the easel. "I've prepared this board the same way I would for one of my paintings. Glue and lead white paint, sanded again and again, until 'tis nearly as flat as canvas. 'Twill hold color better than the canvas, however, and is much sturdier." Her eyes twinkled when she flicked her gaze toward him. "Not only that, but if mistakes are made, 'tis easy to scrape off and start again."

He had to snort again, only this time, the laughter was

rueful. If she expected him to try this, there'd be a hell of a lot of mistakes, he was certain.

"Well, wife?" He held the dish with the malachite toward her. "Let's see ye work yer magic."

Magic? Aye. As he watched the way her eyes lit with joy, he knew this wife of his was indeed worthy of magic. What she was doing, as well as who she was. Pure magic.

As she dipped her fingers into the oil paint, then applied them to the wood, she kept up her talk about form and perspective. And he found himself watching breathlessly as a hillside took shape on the board, complete with waving grasses and small white flowers. Not just any hillside, but— Jaimie found his gaze darting for the open window—a good representation of the view he now saw every day.

"How did ye learn to do that, lass?" he asked with no little amount of reverence in his voice. "'Tis remarkable."

Almost as remarkable as the flushed look of pride she gave him before shrugging off his words.

"When we were young, our priest was a Sinclair who had spent time in a monastery and learned the art of illuminating manuscripts. Some of the nuns from the nearby abbey had participated as well, so Father Mark saw no reason not to teach an impressionable girl what he knew."

Her smile turned wistful as her gaze dropped to the dish of paint in her hands. "I always dreamed of joining that order, of helping to produce illuminated manuscripts which would last for centuries." She shrugged. "But I knew I couldnae give up the chance for…"

When she trailed off, he *had* to know what she'd meant. "The chance for what?" he asked in a choked whisper.

She shrugged again, as if the matter wasn't important. But when she met his gaze, there was a look of fierce yearning in them he'd never seen before.

"All this," she whispered. "A husband. A home. *Bairns.*"

Bairns? She wanted bairns, more than just Callan? If she wanted babes, she wanted to be pregnant, and if she wanted to be pregnant… she wanted to be bedded again.

Bedding her? Nay, he couldn't allow himself to consider that. Best to focus on what she deserved. "And ye found that in yer marriage with David?"

"Nay," she said as she turned back to the easel. "David couldnae give me what I wanted."

"And what is that?" He swallowed, not sure he wanted to hear her answer.

When it came, her voice was so low he was afraid he had imagined it.

"My husband's heart."

Dear God in heaven, if he hadn't been in love with her before, he was now.

It would have been easier to pretend he hadn't heard her, but her bravery deserved a response. He cleared his throat. "Ye deserve all that and more, Agata. I'm sorry I'm not the man—"

Before he could finish, she whirled to face him. "The church says 'tis my duty to give ye bairns, Jaimie Mackenzie." She stepped forward and pointed one green-stained finger at his chest. "My king and my father say 'tis my duty to build a strong alliance through my marriage." She was glaring up at him now. "But I say, if there's one thing I do afore I die, 'tis my duty to prove to ye that *ye are a worthy man.*"

She stepped toward him until the paint on her finger brushed against his linen shirt, but he couldn't make himself care.

"Ye are a worthy man, Jaimie Mackenzie!" Her expression softened. "I dinnae ken what happened in yer past to make ye think ye are not, but I hope one day ye trust me enough to share that story. In the meantime, I will stand afore ye and beside ye, and do my best to prove ye are the man I ken ye to be."

She was breathing heavily as she finished her declaration, and Jaimie realized he was as well. She believed in him? She believed in him so strongly she would make a vow like that?

He shook his head in disbelief.

She nodded in response.

"Yer aunt talks about yer treasure being in the south, aye?" When he nodded, she pressed her finger into his chest. "She's wrong, ye ken. Yer treasure is *here*, and one day ye'll realize it."

Then, before he could argue further, she stepped back and thrust the dish of paint into his hand. "I'll show ye," she declared firmly. "Come."

Unable to deny her, Jaimie stepped toward the easel. As he turned, she took his hand in hers, and placed her fingers over his.

"Like this," she said gently.

With a touch as light as a lover's caress, she showed him how to dip the pad of his thumb into the green paint, and brush it across the board. She stood behind him, the swell of her breasts against him, and he found himself hardly daring to breathe as the opposite side of the valley slowly bloomed beneath their joined fingers. She showed him how to dance across the wood, how to create magic with what was left of his fingers. She showed him how to smear and rub, to bring out shade and sun and the movement of the grasses in the wind. And when she had him dip one of his fingers into the white paint, he somehow forgot how broken he really was.

Jaimie realized she was right. He *was* capable. He'd beaten his cravings for ale, he'd taken over running the clan business, he'd begun training with the men once more.

He was exhausted, overwhelmed, and more than a little scared for the future.

But he was capable. And if *that* was the truth, if she could prove he could do so much more than he'd thought possible, then was she right about his value as well?

Was he worthy of a woman like Agata? A woman whom fate and that old dragon, Aunt Jean, had thrust upon him as his wife?

Jaimie allowed himself to lean back against her, to revel in the strength of her arms and her convictions as she held his hand and taught him how to paint.

Under their joined fingers, the distant valley was appearing, and it was beautiful.

Not as beautiful as his wife, but remarkable because they'd made it together.

She thought he was worthy, and hers was the only opinion which mattered. If that's how she felt, Jaimie knew he had to confess his sins. She might think him worthy now, but would she still believe that when she knew how he had failed Aileen?

Nay, he couldn't think of that now. Not now, not when this trust was still so fragile. Today, he just wanted to enjoy the feeling of his wife's faith. He couldn't confess his sins to her now.

But he'd have to. Soon.

CHAPTER 8

"Be careful, Aunt Agata! There's another spider web up here. Would hate to get it in yer hair again!"

The little boy's cheerful tone belied his warning, so Agata stifled her smile and pretended sternness. "That's why I'm wearing a veil on this adventure." She'd learned her lesson on one of their first excursions into the keep's secret passages. "Besides, ye ken what to do."

Callan gave a little whoop of excitement as he darted forward with the torch, knocking away the long-abandoned web with far too much enthusiasm.

"Go slowly, lad," she cautioned as they set out again.

This was their first chance to explore the entrance Callan had found leading from one of the unused guest rooms on the third story. They'd quickly discovered it connected to one of the other passages in one direction, but by turning right and running along the outer wall, they were in new territory. Agata couldn't help but remember Jaimie's warning about the danger of these passages, so today's exploration was going slower than those in the past, much to Callan's irritation.

"Cannae ye move faster, Aunt Agata? There's light up

ahead!"

Light? That was unexpected.

She was carrying her own candle, so she gathered her skirts in her left hand in a futile attempt to keep them out of the dust. "Lead on, then," she urged.

The passage was extremely narrow with stone on one side —the outer wall—and wood on the other. There was wood beneath their feet, and Agata suspected some past renovation of the keep had walled up this space and it had been forgotten. Was it really as dangerous as Jaimie had said?

"There's something…"

The concentration in the boy's tone cut through Agata's musings. "What?"

She hadn't allowed Callan to get more than two paces ahead of her, so when he held the torch up to the wooden wall to their right, she could immediately see the markings he meant, and her heart leapt with excitement.

"Look, Aunt Agata! There's some kind of writing here. Is it a clue?"

A clue! At last, a clue to what happened to the Sinclair jewels so long ago!

She reached him before he was done speaking, and they both leaned in to examine the wall by the light of their flames. Callan's hand was pressed flat against the wood, but Agata's eyes were all that skimmed over the marks burned into the wood.

After the initial excitement, she sighed with disappointment and straightened.

"'Tis just the builder's mark, lad." She pointed to the simple straight lines intersecting the letters. "They must've branded the wood afore they put up this wall."

The boy slumped against the stone, clearly not caring how dusty he got, and muttered a curse he probably shouldn't have known yet. "I really thought we'd found a clue. Although I dinnae see why ye cannae tell me what kind of clue we *are* looking for."

She reached out and ruffled his dark hair, not even minding the dirt in it. "If I kenned what we were looking for, I'd tell ye. All I ken is that 'tis a piece of Sinclair history."

Actually, that wasn't *all* she knew. She knew the clue they were looking for would lead them to the location of the missing jewels… but she couldn't tell the lad that. For one thing, the idea of jewels and treasure might send him off into the passages on his own, and although he was used to poking around unsupervised, her husband's warning last week had made her unwilling to allow the boy into the passages alone.

But more than the boy, she regretted not being able to tell *Jaimie*. He nearly admitted he'd explored the passages in his youth, so *surely* if there was a clue to be found, he would know of it? And even more than that, she wanted to tell him because he was her husband. And the more time she spent with him, the more she wanted to share *everything* with him.

Not just about her search for a clue to the jewels, but about what she held in her heart.

Because the longer she was married to him, the more certain she was that she was falling in love with this man.

When they'd first met, her heart had broken for the pain and anguish she'd seen in him, pain even the drink couldn't hide. Now that he'd broken the drink's hold on him, she was falling in love with his unexpected strength and pride. He'd overcome so much, but was still so humble, he thought himself unworthy of praise.

She wondered what he thought about her words yesterday, when she'd stood in the solar and allowed her frustrations out. She'd meant every word; he was worthy of happiness, worthy of love, and she planned on doing her best to convince him.

Taking a deep breath, she nodded to Callan to continue on, full of determination. Determination to find the clues they needed, and determination to teach this husband of hers how she felt.

"Look, Aunt Agata!"

When the boy darted forward in excitement, she almost scolded him, but held her tongue when she saw the same thing he had. Up ahead, the source of the light they'd seen early was a pair of arrow slits in the stone outer wall. She hurried ahead to join him in peering out them.

"They must've been walled up when they renovated this wing," she explained, careful to keep the candle out of the gentle breeze wafting past the openings, knowing she'd need it later.

"I cannae see aught," Callan complained, standing on his tip-toes. "Just the sky."

"I dinnae ken—"

The words died in her throat when she pressed her face to the stone in an effort to see more than what Callan could. Since she was taller, she was able to look down into the field beside the keep...where the men were training.

"What do ye see, Aunt Agata?" the lad asked desperately.

"Naught," she answered distractedly. "Just the men training."

Aye, the men were training. And aye, the Mackenzie warriors were an impressive bunch, but they weren't what held her attention. Nay, that honor went to the shirtless man standing among the circle of cheering warriors, sparring with a grizzled opponent.

Jaimie spun and leapt with an unbelievable grace.

From where she stood, she had a full view of their battle. They weren't using mock swords, but the heavy blades her father's men had trained with as well. The summer sun glistened off the sweat streaking Jaimie's shoulders and back, and when he whirled out of the way of one of his opponent's strikes, his kilt parted with an intriguing view of one of his thighs. Although he wasn't as broad as the older warrior, he was more agile, that was clear.

His opponent swung for his head, the smartest target, and rather than blocking it, Jaimie swept his right foot to the side, and at the last moment, ducked and shifted his weight so the other warrior's sword passed above him. Suddenly, he was within the man's reach, and Agata caught her breath when she realized how effortlessly he'd made it look.

In the time it took her to blink, Jaimie had shifted his grip on his sword and swung it, catching his opponent across the stomach with the flat of the blade. The circle of warriors broke into cheers as the other man folded over and went down. Agata found herself bouncing lightly on her toes in excitement as well.

"What is it, Aunt Agata? What's down there?"

"Hmm?" She shook herself. "Oh, naught important. Let us…"

She made the mistake of glancing back down again, and saw Jaimie leaning down to help the other man up. They were both laughing, and the way Jaimie clasped forearms with the warrior—as well as the respect on the faces of the men around them—told Agata that whatever his past failings, the Mackenzie warriors had forgiven Jaimie.

He'd found acceptance, and that was important to her campaign to prove him worthy.

At that moment, Jaimie threw his head back in laughter at something one of the gathered men had said, and the sun caused the skin of his throat to glisten. His hair fell away from his face, and she saw *pride* there.

It was appealing.

"*Agata*," Callan whined again.

"We have to go… um, back." She straightened and nodded to the boy. "We have to go down. Now. Immediately."

Despite the boy's protests, she shooed him back in the

direction they came. All she could care about at the moment was the way Jaimie had looked, satisfied and proud and covered in sweat.

Oh dear, mayhap he needed someone to wash his hair again? She realized she was already considering what needed to be done to order him a bath.

"But this passageway was the best one yet," Callan was complaining as they hurried to retrace their steps toward the chamber where they'd entered it. "There might've been a clue—"

"We'll come back, I promise. Tomorrow morning, first thing." Then, even her limited experience with an inquisitive and fearless seven-year-old boy overrode the breathless excitement of seeing Jaimie again, so she hastened to add, "But together, aye? Remember what yer uncle said about the dangers."

The boy scoffed. "'Tis no' dangerous. Unless ye think spiders are dangerous."

She poked him in the side with a finger, causing him to squirm. "*I* dinnae like them."

"Ye better no' be mean to me, then," he mumbled.

She poked him again, with genuine affection. "I heard that. If ye think to put a spider in my bed, wee one, I'll tell Cook to prepare goose for a sennight straight."

The boy groaned at the threat—he hated goose—and increased his pace until they came to the wooden panel he'd discovered. They had to shift together to get back into the guest chamber. Once there, they doused their candle and torch, and she sent him back to his nurse with instructions to wash his hands and face, and maybe the old woman wouldn't notice the dust over the rest of him.

Although she'd have to be blind not to; they both looked as if they'd been… well, as if they'd been crawling through the spaces between the walls of the keep.

She didn't even bother to take her own advice as she yanked off her veil and pulled up her skirts and rushed down the stone stairs and through the great hall. She didn't see Jean until she stepped out of the stairwell and pulled up short.

"Where are ye off to in such a hurry?"

Agata gave a hurried curtsey and a wry grin. "Nowhere in particular, Aunt Jean. I just thought to enjoy the beautiful weather a bit…"

"Hmm." The older woman nodded knowingly. "And the fact the warriors are all out in the courtyard congratulating yer husband on a victory—that has naught to do with it?"

Agata's eyes widened with feigned innocence. "Oh, is Jaimie outside? I had no idea." She ducked her head to hide her grin, and tried to squeeze past Jean. "Please excuse me."

But her aunt wasn't fooled, judging from the laughter which escaped the other woman. "Aye, go on to him," she said fondly. "But would ye like me to order a bath in his chamber?"

Already on the first step leading to the armory, Agata remembered her earlier plan. "Oh, would ye?"

"Aye, lass," Jean said gently. "I'll make sure there's enough water for both of ye." She winked and nodded toward Agata's dust-covered gown. "Maybe Jaimie can wash *yer* back this time."

Agata had no idea how the wily old woman had learned of Jaimie's last bath and how wonderfully it had brought her and Jaimie together. But she just laughed and waved her thanks before reaching for her skirts once more.

She hurried down the steps and through the armory, then burst out of the main door. The bright sun caused her to wince, but she didn't stop. She had no idea why she was so consumed with excitement. But seeing Jaimie's pride—and his sweat-slick body—had kindled a need deep inside her, and today she was determined to see her dream of love fulfilled.

THE FIGHT HAD Jaimie's blood pumping, but knocking Owen on his arse had been more thrilling than Jaimie had remembered. He wanted to throw his head back and howl in victory, but instead, he laughed with the other men and helped his opponent up off the ground, accepting the accolades and ribbing as his due.

"Good to have ye back, milord," a panting Owen had said as the older warrior clapped him on the shoulder. "Yer sword arm isnae any worse for wear."

"Aye!" called another warrior. "If ye can knock Owen like that, I'll gladly follow ye into battle if the Sutherlands get ambitious again!"

The gathered men roared with laughter at that, calling back challenges and threats and predictions, and a warmth spread throughout Jaimie. It was acceptance and happiness and...

And *pride*.

These men, these warriors, had always been David's, and Jaimie had trained as one of them throughout his youth. He'd gone away to the Grant holding, where he'd met Aileen, then to court. By the time he'd returned home, he was no longer one of them.

But now...

Ye are worthy.

Agata had said that, and hearing the men's acceptance and knowing he'd won their praise, Jaimie was beginning to believe it.

"Hey, Owen!" Wee Thomas yelled as he slapped the older man on the back of the head. "Ye smell like a ram fucked a cow! Ye best wash afore Margery catches a wiff o' ye!"

Owen grabbed for the lad, who ducked out of the way, laughing.

"Ye've got nae place to talk," Owen growled, lunging again. "I'll throw ye in the loch myself!"

As the two chased through the outer walls, the rest of the men laughed and ribbed one another. "An' ye, milord?" one of them called to Jaimie. "Ye'll join us afore that pretty new wife of yers catches wind o' ye?"

Jaimie swallowed and nodded, not sure he trusted himself to speak. He was nigh overwhelmed with pride at their acceptance.

"Och, nevermind," another called. "'Tis too late."

The men roared with mirth and made their way toward the distant loch, but Jaimie didn't go with them. Nay, his attention was stolen by what they'd seen, Agata, her skirt hiked up as she rushed toward him, her honey-gold hair streaming behind her, and an expression of intense *joy* on her face.

"Husband!" she called as she skidded to a stop before him, breathless and brilliant. "I saw yer victory from—" She made a vague motion toward one of the windows of the upper stories. "*Magnificent.*"

Nay, it was her smile which was magnificent, and made Jaimie feel as if he were the most important man in the world. Still, he couldn't seem to make his throat work, but merely nodded, entranced by her joy and beauty.

She took a step forward, and although her smile didn't lessen, it did *change* somewhat, as well as the light in her eyes, until he could swear she looked... well, seductive. She looked as if she wanted something, and knew how to go about getting it.

He took a deep breath and prayed he could be the one to give it to her.

Her hand rose to his cheek, and he was proud he didn't flinch when her fingertips brushed against his scarred skin as she brushed his hair behind his ear.

"Ye look hot, Jaimie," she murmured, her eyes searching his face, then dropping lower to his chest. "Will ye let me wash ye?"

Beneath his kilt, his cock twitched at the memory of the last bath he'd enjoyed, and how he'd imagined her there with him. Although her gaze was still fastened on his chest, he jerked his chin down in a nod. "Aye."

Her fingers twined through his, and that now-familiar warmth spread up his arm. She tugged him toward the keep—away from the loch, but at that moment he didn't care—and Jaimie knew he'd follow her anywhere she commanded.

Which is how he found himself standing in the middle of her room, his eyes following her movements as she poured water from an ewer to a basin, then carefully dipped in a cloth. The last time he'd been here, he'd woken with her wrapped in his arms, his cock hard enough to cut stone. And although Callan had interrupted whatever had been building between them, it hadn't been that bad. It'd made Jaimie feel as if they were a family.

"Come here," Agata called softly, and Jaimie felt his feet move before he'd realized it.

When he reached the small table in front of the window, Agata wrung the water from the cloth and lifted it. When its coolness pressed against his forehead, he sucked in a startled breath, but couldn't quite tamp down the sigh of pleasure which escaped his lips.

At the sound, her expression softened and she dragged the cloth across his cheek, pushing his hair behind his shoulder, and sponging his neck and collarbone.

He realized he was holding his breath as she wet the cloth again and wiped the sweat from the other side of his jaw and collarbone. God Almighty, but it felt good to be taken care of this way.

Closing his eyes, he surrendered to the sensation. Not the

pleasure of the cool cloth or her gentle hands necessarily, but the knowledge someone cared. *She* cared.

When her hands moved away, it took a moment before he opened his eyes. She'd put the cloth down, but was turning back to him with something in her hands—a leather tie? Before he could ask about it, she reached up and wrapped her arms around his neck.

Jaimie had stiffened in surprise before he realized what she was doing. She gathered his hair and secured it with the tie so it hung down his back instead of in his face.

But when she was through, she didn't pull away. Nay, instead, she rested with her arms around his neck, watching him.

"There," she whispered. "I've wanted to do that for a while."

He tried to clear his throat, but couldn't force any sound out. He didn't even know what to say. Instead, cautiously, he lifted his hands from where they hung by his side and slowly, gently, rested them on her hips.

And she smiled.

They stood there, her arms around his neck, his hands on her hips, and it seemed *so comfortable*. As if the universe—as if God Himself—were showing Jaimie how life could be.

He'd promised himself he wouldn't push her. Wouldn't take her the way he had on their wedding night. Nay, he wanted to wait until she *gave* herself to him, until she told him to take her, but... but the look in her eyes, the heavy-lidded look of breathless anticipation, told Jaimie she was as aroused as he was.

He knew passion when he saw it.

"Lass," he whispered roughly. "I wanted ye to have control of this, but..."

It wasn't his imagination that she sucked in a breath. "Aye?"

Please God, let her say she yearns for this as well.

"Agata... I'm going to kiss ye."

She groaned in surrender and dropped her head back. "Aye, Jaimie! Now, if ye please."

He didn't even stop to smile at her pert command. Instead, his lips brushed against hers, then again, then…

Then he just stopped and savored the feel of a woman's lips on his, barely touching, the taste and smell and *nearness* of her. It'd been years since a woman had allowed him to kiss her, and this was no mere woman.

This was Agata!

Under his gentle touch, she made a little noise of frustration and shifted her weight. She tugged him closer. He didn't bother fighting, but lost himself in her touch.

And when her lips opened of their own accord, Jaimie's tongue swept between them as if it were the most natural thing in the world. She moaned against his lips and pulled him even closer, until she was leaning back and his arms were around her slim waist supporting her. Their tongues danced erotically, and he remembered all the times he'd imagined her like this.

The reality was even better.

God only knew how long they kissed before he backed her into the table. The basin clattered against the ewer. He pulled away from her with a gasp, reaching for the pottery, but she kept her arms locked firmly around him.

They were both breathing frantically as they met each other's gazes.

"Agata," he breathed, his throat tight and his cock thick against his thigh. He couldn't think of aught more to say than, "*Agata,*" again.

She loosened her hold long enough to place one palm against his cheek. "Why do ye cover this?"

It hadn't been what he'd expected her to say, not after she'd allowed him to kiss her. "What?" he asked, rearing away from her touch.

She followed. "I wish ye'd wear yer hair pulled back, Jaimie. I'll have special ties made for ye, or ye can use mine." Her fingers stroked his cheek once more. "Then ye willnae be able to hide."

He swallowed. If she wanted that—if she commanded him—he would shave his head as bald as his chin. But a habit of many years was hard to break.

"If I wear it pulled back…"

"Aye?" she prompted gently.

And he knew she already suspected what he would say. "Then everyone will see… see my scar."

But she just shook her head slightly. "Ye dinnae want them to see *ye*, Jaimie. Why is that?"

"Because I used to be handsome!" he blurted.

Then, ashamed of his weakness, he tried to pull out of her arms once more, the kiss nigh forgotten in what she was asking from him. But Agata was stronger than he was, and didn't release him. Instead, she just smiled gently.

"Ye still are, husband."

Handsome? He snorted.

She continued. "I find ye handsome, and I'm the only one who matters, aye? Besides, regardless of what ye're saying now, I dinnae think ye're so vain as to be ashamed over a little scar."

"Little—?" he repeated. Could she really be so blind? He held up his hands in front of her, trying to frighten her. "Is this so little, eh? I lost my fingers, Agata!"

She merely nodded and dropped her hold to his hands. When he should have stepped away from her—away from this room and the things she was making him feel—she tightened her hold on him, twining her fingers through his.

"Aye, ye did. Will ye tell me what happened?"

"Nay."

"Jaimie, ye are a good man. I ken ye're ashamed, but I dinnae ken why. Will ye tell me?"

Ashamed. She was wrong. He wasn't a good man. He closed his eyes tightly, hating how gently she was asking him.

But in only a few short weeks, she'd come to know him better than anyone. She knew he could resist a plea, but when she hardened her voice, he was powerless.

"Jaimie," she commanded. "Tell me."

He couldn't deny her.

But he couldn't tell her while looking at her. He jerked away again, and this time she let him go. Facing the window, he forced his eyes open and scrubbed his hand across his face.

"There was a woman."

It was a start, at least. Behind him, she made a little noise of encouragement, and he heard her move across the chamber. Somehow, it was easier when she was further away. Further from his shame.

"I fostered with the Grants, her family, and I thought..." He shook his head and took a deep breath. "I loved her. I'd kenned her for years, and she gave herself to me." He hadn't been her first, but it didn't matter. Not when he'd been so passionate for her. "Even after I went to court and bedded other women, she was the one I kept coming back to."

She was the one who'd held his heart, who'd enjoyed the power over him.

Agata's voice was soft when she asked, "What happened?"

With a muffled curse, he turned from the window and snatched up the cloth she'd dropped. Throwing it into the basin, he didn't even bother wringing it out before he slapped it against his shoulder, viciously rubbing at the sweat and dirt from the training session.

"Tell me."

His hand stilled and he closed his eyes. God in Heaven, she knew what he needed. Her urging loosened something inside of him, allowed him to breathe again. Jaimie forced himself say the words.

"I visited her family, and she came to my bed. I pleasured her... and the next morning, she told me she was to be married to my brother."

Agata's startled gasp was eclipsed by a crash. Jaimie swung around to see her skirts sway around her and a small wooden chair on its side behind her. She'd stood up so suddenly she'd knocked it over? And judging from the way her hands were fisted by her side, she was furious.

"*Aileen*," she hissed.

He nodded, his heart breaking again, knowing he'd caused her pain, mentioning David. "Aileen would never be satisfied with me, not when David was laird. I ken that now," he mumbled as he began to slowly wipe down his arms. "She married him the following day, and I returned to court."

"Jaimie," she whispered, and he hated the pity he heard in her voice. He'd pitied himself too damn much over the last years. Swallowing, he turned away, concentrating on the cold water and cloth.

"She kept sending me messages, inviting me to visit. Callan was born nine months after their wedding, and I—" He felt his throat closing up at the memory. "I had to see the lad."

Suddenly, she was beside him once more, but didn't touch him. "He's yers?" she asked in a rough whisper.

He shook his head, then lifted one shoulder in a hopeless shrug. "He has the Mackenzie eyes, but Aileen's hair was as dark as mine. He could be David's."

It was the not-knowing part which had kept him away for so long, only to drag him back in moments of weakness. Aileen had never told him the truth, but laughed and waved away his questions as if they hadn't mattered. And maybe they *hadn't*. David had thought the lad was his son, and Callan would be the next Mackenzie laird, assuming his regent didn't fail him.

That's when Agata touched him again. "He could be, and he has yer spirit, Jaimie. Yer love, yer passions."

He squeezed his eyes shut. She was right, just as she'd been that day outside the walls, when he'd gone looking for them and she'd told him how much Callan needed him. The lad had needed to know it was fine to grow up *feeling* and expressing himself, rather than the way David had been... because Callan was so very much like Jaimie himself.

And, as he'd told himself before, he would raise Callan as if it didn't matter. Maybe the lad was David's. Maybe he was Jaimie's. But either way, he was the next Mackenzie laird, and Jaimie *loved him*.

"Will ye..." She hesitated, then continued. "Will ye tell me what happened to ye, Jaimie?"

He'd oblige her, since he'd come so far already.

Cold water dripped down his arms, and he tossed the now-dirty cloth back into the basin. The breeze from the window caused his skin to prickle with awareness, and he bit down on a shiver.

"She begged me to come for Yule when the lad was four. I took him riding," he admitted, the memory a happy one.

"I remember Callan saying that," she said encouragingly. "'Tis good he has such fond memories."

Jaimie's nod was more of a quick jerk, and suddenly, he was desperate to get it all said. "I confronted Aileen once more, and we quarreled. She accused me of no' really loving her, and by that time..."

He shook his head. He'd realized what he felt for Aileen had been a yearning, while she'd had some kind of *need* to be in control of him. It could have been wonderfully freeing, to grant her control... but by then, he knew he couldn't trust her.

Not the way he trusted Agata.

He tried again. "Now I ken she saw her control over me slipping, and that upset her more than my feelings did. She said…" He took a deep breath and shot a glance at Agata before looking away. "She said if I didnae love her, she'd rather die. I thought she was being dramatic, so when she ran out into the night, I didnae bother telling David."

"Ye followed her." Agata's fingers tightened around his upper arm.

It hadn't been a question, but he nodded. "Aye, I followed her. It wasnae snowing, but it was bitter cold. I couldnae see her, but I could hear her, laughing, calling to me." His voice dropped to a whisper. "Telling me it was my fault she wasnae in the warmth where she belonged."

He remembered that. He remembered her mocking words, but they were impossible, because…

"But by the time I found her, she was frozen. She'd fallen down a bank and hit her head. It was hours later, and she was damn near solid. I… I remember being near frozen, too." He'd put his cheek against hers, had gathered her face in his hands, and had wept.

Agata's hand slid down his wet arm to his hand. "That scar…ye told me 'twas a cold burn, aye? Ye sat there with her body and allowed the cold to scar ye?"

He stared down at their hands, his fingers barely longer than hers now. "Aye," he whispered. "It seemed appropriate."

"And ye think ye failed her. Ye think ye're the reason she's dead."

Again, it wasn't a question, but he nodded, unable to speak.

"Ye feel shame because she's dead?"

Her faintly skeptical tone forced his gaze up to hers. There was something sparkling in those warm brown depths, and the knowledge irritated him.

"Her death was my fault, aye. I cost Callan his mother, and

David his wife. And myself…" His voice caught, but he pushed on. "It cost me my—my pride."

She scoffed. "Ye're being vain again, Jaimie. Yer ability to woo the court ladies wasnae—"

"*Vain?*" The word exploded out of his mouth like a curse. "Is it *vain* to mourn the loss of my hands, lass?" His fingers tightened on hers. "I lost my ability to—"

"To *what*, husband?" she snapped in a suddenly firm voice. She stepped closer, her body—her *breasts*—pressed against his side. "To write? To wield a bow? To *paint*?" She pushed herself up on her tiptoes. "To woo a woman?" she whispered in his ear.

And more than the picture those words conjured, it was the challenge in her voice which made Jaimie's eyes narrow. He dropped his chin so his lips were even with hers.

"Ye saw me wield a sword and taught me to paint, lass. Are ye doubting my abilities in *other areas?*"

When her eyes flashed with victory, he realized he'd walked right into her trap. And he didn't mind one damn bit.

"Prove it," she challenged.

The knock on the door made both of them jump, but they didn't pull apart.

"My lady, the bath ye requested—oh!" Morag, the little serving wench with the limp, blushed and glanced at the floor when she saw the two of them standing so close. "I mean… yer bath is ready, laird. I mean, *milord*. I mean…"

Flustered, she curtseyed and backed out of the room. Jaimie watched her go, but when he turned back to his wife, Agata was watching him with a speculative look.

"What?" he snapped.

She grinned. "I'm going to prove ye're still the man ye remember. Follow me."

CHAPTER 9

AGATA LIKED that he didn't resist as she tugged him into his room, then shut the door behind him. Just as in her chambers, he stood in the middle of the room and watched her warily. He wasn't quite sure what her plan was, and that empowered her.

This was it. This was the moment she would show him who he was.

The bath steamed in front of the hearth, the scented oils perfuming the air. This room was smaller than hers. She'd only been in here a few times since her return as Lady Mackenzie, and had decided she liked it much more than the laird's chambers. As she strolled toward the hearth, she pondered the possibility of moving her things in here to be with him.

Because the more she got to know Jaimie, the more she realized she would be quite delighted to spend the rest of her life curled up with him in bed.

And after today, he'd know it, too.

Turning, she met his gaze, reached up, and began to untie

her gown. She made fast work of the laces, and soon the midnight-blue wool was hanging low on her shoulders.

His hands slowly fisted at his sides as he watched, and although his breathing was slow and even, it was a little too deliberate, as if he was forcing himself to stay calm. Which is why she allowed her desire to show in her smile.

Mayhap she was a better seductress than she'd imagined, because he sucked in a breath and his tongue traced his lower lip as his nostrils flared. The memory of their first kiss—how long she'd waited to kiss him—made heat pool in her belly.

She held his gaze as she pushed her gown down over her shoulders and wriggled out of it, kicking it and her slippers aside. Her chemise was just as modest as the gown had been, but she noticed the way his eyes dropped to her breasts. Was he remembering the way she'd placed her breasts in his hands? Was he looking forward to doing it again?

It was difficult to tamp down the giggle which almost crawled up her throat, but she did. Stripping in front of him made her feel powerful. She didn't *need* power over Jaimie, not the way Aileen obviously had… and she cared too much about him to ever hurt him. But she was in charge, as he'd said he'd wanted.

"Jaimie, take off yer boots."

He nodded and bent to pull off his shoes. When he straightened, he met her eyes once more with a look which was part challenge, part yearning.

So, she rewarded him with an approving nod. "Good. Now yer kilt."

He hesitated a moment longer, but his hands eventually moved to his buckle. He made short work of it, and as he dropped it on the floor, the tartan around his hips sagged, held up only by his hands clasped in front of him. Unlike their wedding night, he wasn't wearing a shirt, but he hadn't been this modest the night she'd washed his hair.

"Jaimie," she cajoled with another smile.

His chin came up, and with a sudden breath, he let the kilt fall.

It was her time to suck in a delighted gasp. He was perfect to her. Three years of hard living and drink hadn't destroyed his body. In the weeks they'd been married, he'd trained with the men as often as possible. His shoulders were broader and his stomach more defined than on their wedding night. With his hair pulled back, she could see the pride and challenge and *intensity* in his expression.

Well, she was *quite* pleased with her husband, and nearly breathless for what was to come. He wasn't as big as David had been, but Jaimie's stomach tapered to narrow hips which emphasized his member dragging her attention downward. It jutted straight out from its nest of thick hair, and as she watched, it grew larger and harder, until it stood up straight against his belly.

Goodness, it certainly was *long*, wasn't it?

It was taking all her concentration not to press her thighs together to relieve the fierce ache at her core.

Soon, she promised herself.

Knowing that Jaimie was waiting, she let her approval show. "Ye are magnificent."

His neck flexed as he swallowed. "God's blood, Agata," he choked out in a rough whisper. "Ye're damn near killing me."

"Aye, ye've done verra well sharing so much of yerself with me. Ye deserve a reward."

Her hands were already by her sides, so she began to gather her chemise, inching it up her legs. She revealed her stocking-clad legs, but she halted her movements when the linen material was bunched right below her hips. She loved the way his gaze was riveted on what had already been revealed, and he could barely contain himself.

Smiling, she lifted the chemise over her head and was soon standing there in naught but her stockings.

He groaned and took one jerking step forward, as if pulled by an invisible string, but managed to stop. When his eyes met hers once more, there was a *hunger* there which made her feel very wanted.

She stretched her arms toward him, and the silent permission was all he needed. He was on her in a flash, and only hesitated a moment before wrapping his arms around her. She gasped at the sensation of his long member pressed against her belly, and she couldn't help the way she wiggled against him, the pressure sending all sorts of delightful sparks through her.

But as much as she was ready to feel him inside her again, that wasn't what he needed.

He needed confidence. He needed to see himself the way she saw him.

So, she stroked the hairs at the back of his neck and whispered, "Pleasure me, Jaimie."

Something flashed in his dark blue eyes.

She smiled in encouragement. "Pleasure me until I beg."

With a groan of surrender, he lowered his lips to hers, then quickly moved to her jaw and neck. After the way he'd kissed her in her chambers, this was... this was everything she and her sisters had ever discussed and more. She sighed and dropped her head back, allowing him better access to her collarbone, where he nibbled.

One of his hands was pressed to her back, and the other dropped to her breast. Jaimie cupped it, then pulled back just enough to stare down at her.

Agata moaned low in her throat and shifted on her feet in an effort to relieve the delicious ache between her legs.

It must've been all the encouragement Jaimie needed, because he hummed and lowered his mouth to her breast, nipping gently at the bud with his teeth. When his tongue rasped across the sensitive part again, she whispered his name.

He kept his hand on her, but moved his attention to her other breast, drawing the nipple into his mouth. She bent further to give him better access. With a growl, he pushed her back as he stepped with her, and before she understood what had happened, she was lying on his bed with him leaning over her.

"Jaimie," she whimpered, squirming against the coverlet. Instinctively, her legs opened, and she had to press her hands into the mattress to keep from reaching for him and urging him inside her.

Not yet. Soon.

"Is that ye begging, lass?" he growled.

"Nay!" she gasped, writhing. "No' yet."

The right corner of his mouth lifted in a wicked grin. "I'll persevere."

He knelt between her legs—as he'd done on their wedding night, but this time, mutual passion ruled their hearts. His hands closed possessively around her breasts and he leaned down. He placed soft kisses against the skin near one nipple, then the other, reaching the valley between them. His thumb brushed against her nipples. When his lips reached her breastbone, he pushed both mounds together until the faint whiskers on his cheeks scraped her sensitive skin. In response, she arched.

"Jaimie!"

"No' yet," he said.

As she forced herself to be patient, he trailed kisses down her stomach, circling her navel with his tongue before going lower.

She was so caught up in the anticipation, she barely noticed when his hands left her breasts to trail down her sides and grasped her hips. It wasn't until he slid from between her legs to kneel on the floor that she realized what he was going to do.

Lifting herself on her elbows, she was just in time to see him lower his face to her inner thighs, and gasped when he nipped gently. Instinctively, she spread her legs wider and *loved* the way his gaze was immediately drawn to her womanhood.

"God Almighty, lass," he whispered. "Ye're wet already."

"Aye, husband, for *ye*."

He needed to understand that he alone was responsible for her excitement. His eyes flashed to hers, and aye, there was passion in their dark depths and pride, too.

It was the most attractive she'd ever felt, watching him prepare to pleasure her. Oh, she'd touched herself, knew how to find release. But *this*? Knowing a man wanted her enough, *cared* for her enough to bring her pleasure? And knowing she could watch him as he did…? That was the purest form of confidence in herself.

Slowly, reverently, he leaned forward until his breath tickled her curls. Then his thumbs spread her, revealing her most intimate spot.

He groaned with desperation.

She dropped back against the mattress as his thumb pressed against her nub of pleasure and he kissed and licked her core.

She raised her hips, desperate for *something* more—something that would bring them closer.

Pressure built within her as his thumb worked against her most sensitive spot. She was going to…

"Nay!" she gasped, raising up so she could see him. "I want to feel yer fingers inside me, please!"

"Shh, lass," he whispered, urging her back once more.

She relented, but he didn't let her look away. Nay, he held her captive with his intense stare and the way his fingers moved over her flesh. Her breaths came more rapidly, erratically.

That's when he slipped one finger inside her, and she cried out.

"That's it, lass," he coaxed, using the heel of his hand to rub her pearl as he stroked with his thumb. "That's it, Agata. Come for me."

"Oh, Jaimie."

He slipped another finger inside her, and she writhed and closed her eyes.

"I can feel ye," he whispered hoarsely. "Soft and tight around me. Ye want me inside ye, wife? Ye want to feel my cock deep in here." He moved his fingers, and her hips bucked. "Ye're *aching* for me, Agata."

"Aye," she moaned.

"Say it, wife. Beg me."

She was too deep in the throes of passion to deny him. "*Please*, Jaimie."

With a cry, she felt herself hurtling toward the clouds, the sweet pressure building beyond what she could imagine. The sensations, they were—they were…

"Come for me, wife."

She screamed his name as she let go, bursting apart. She felt his lips on her once more, his fingers continuing to tease and fulfill her every need.

She was *flying*.

And then, she felt him withdraw, felt the mattress lurch as he climbed onto the bed. His hands were on her hips, her stomach, her breasts, before she was able to force her eyes open, her insides still spasming and her breath coming fast and heavy from the strength of her climax.

He braced one hand over her shoulder, the other stroking his length the way he had on their wedding night. Except this time, the look on his face wasn't anger, but a hunger so deep, she couldn't wait another moment.

"Agata," he whispered, and she knew what he was asking.

She repositioned her legs, knees bent, inviting him inside her. The relief on his face was evident as he grabbed onto her hips and plunged inside her with a powerful thrust.

Oh, yes.

He groaned and dropped his forehead to the crook of her neck.

"What are ye doing?" she panted, desperate to capture that marvelous sensation once more. Why wasn't he moving?

When he lifted his head, his grin was downright devilish. "Waiting for ye to *beg*, wife."

The sound which escaped her lips was part laugh, part moan, and all joy. *"Please!"* she managed to gasp.

Taking pity on her, he slid out just a fraction, then plunged home once more. Taking him to the hilt, she arched her back, reveling in the sensations as her hands scrambled at his shoulders. As he worked within her, she wrapped her legs around his hips, urging him to pump harder. His breaths came faster and faster, a grunt escaping his lips each time he slammed into her.

His eyes were filled with wonder. His fierce desperation sent her spiraling to release again. They moved together as if they had done this a thousand times before—a perfect fit.

As if knowing exactly what she needed, Jaimie took all of his weight on one hand, and reached between them to stroke her pearl.

"Aye, lass," he growled, his eyes not leaving hers. "Come for me again."

"Jaimie!"

Her entire body burst with pleasure. He tossed his head back and roared her name as he bucked against her, filling her with the most delicious warmth.

Eventually he rolled to one side, pulling her into his arms.

Her head was tucked under his chin, one of her legs thrown over his thighs.

Their breathing evened out, and she drew small circles on his chest while he absently played with her hair. Finally, she figured she'd waited long enough.

"Ye ken," she said in a low voice against his skin, "I've never done that afore."

He lifted his head to look down at her, so she pulled away to meet his gaze, making sure all of her sincerity and pleasure showed.

"Never done what?" he asked with a frown. "Surely ye've…"

"Aye," she agreed, knowing what he was asking. "I've found pleasure. And I've been bedded." She smiled a little shyly. "But never both together."

He sucked in a breath, his brows shooting up in surprise.

Nodding, she lifted herself up on one elbow to gaze down at him. Her hair had fallen out of its plait and tumbled over one of her shoulders. Her hand wandered down his body and to his manhood.

He stopped her exploration and growled, "*Agata*."

"I've *never* been bedded by a man who cared for my pleasure, husband. Ye're the first to bring me such joy."

He didn't immediately react. In fact, she held her breath, willing him to understand what she was trying to tell him. The confusion in his eyes slowly turned to pride, and a smile brightened his face.

She nodded encouragingly and pulled her hand away to poke him in his chest. "*Ye* did that, Jaimie Mackenzie. And do ye ken what else?"

Without waiting for him to answer, she leaned down and placed her lips beside his ear. "Ye did it with yer *fingers*," she whispered.

A laugh burst out of him and he reached for her, but she rolled away, her laughter joining his. They ended up on the other side of the bed, but he eventually pinned her with his body, looming over her as he grinned down at her.

"Ye were right," he admitted. "I *did* do that."

She clasped his hips, holding him in place. "I've said time and again ye're still the same man ye were three years ago, Jaimie, and I'm pleased to be able to prove it to ye."

His expression turned thoughtful just before he lowered his lips to hers. The kiss was sweet and full of promise.

When he pulled back, there was something *else* in his eyes. Something she couldn't identify, but which seemed important.

"Agata, I—"

She felt as if they'd been on the verge of something important. "Aye?"

He shook his head, as if to chase away whatever thought he'd been having before grinning down at her once more.

"I was wondering how in the hell ye managed to get so dirty. I've been training, aye, but *ye* looked as if ye've been chasing cobwebs all morning!"

Without giving her a chance to explain, he rolled off her. "Come, wife." He pulled her to her feet.

Her eyes widened as he twined his fingers through hers and led her toward the still-steaming bath. "What do ye have in mind?" she asked a little breathlessly.

He grinned over his shoulder. "'Tis time I washed *yer* hair."

A stab of disappointment went through her. "Oh. Ye want me to take a bath? Alone?"

His hand still in hers, he stepped into the tub and tugged her closer. "Nay. I have all sorts of ideas of things to try *together* in here, and I'm determined to try all of them."

And as she sunk into the deliciously warm water in front of him, Agata sighed, part in pleasure, part in anticipation. Because that had very much sounded like a promise.

CHAPTER 10

Jaimie woke face-down on his bed, his legs spread in one direction, his arms in another. He groaned as he rolled onto his side. He felt like warm butter, every muscle relaxed, and he couldn't recall the last time he'd slept so well.

No, that wasn't true. He'd slept just as well the time he'd woken with his arms around his wife, and for the same reason.

Agata had been… *amazing.*

Where was she? Although he knew she wasn't in bed with him, he forced his head up to look around the chamber. No Agata. He flopped back on the pillows with a satisfied sigh, deciding wherever she'd gotten to this morning, he wasn't too concerned. Judging from the angle of the sun through the window, he'd slept late, but—a self-satisfied grin tugged at his lips—he deserved it.

After he'd brought her to climax *twice,* they'd climbed into the tub. Remembering what he'd fantasized about the last time he'd stroked himself, Jaimie had held her between his legs as he'd washed her hair…then her breasts and everything else he could reach, until she was hot and begging for release.

He glanced at the tub. Most of the water had ended up on the floor, come to think of it.

After their relaxing soak, the chatelaine had sent up supper on a tray, and Jaimie didn't think he could ever recall a more perfect meal, curled up naked in bed, feeding one another bread and cheeses and sipping on wine while they spoke of their plans for the future.

Speaking of plans… Jaimie propped the pillows behind his head as he reached for a piece of the now-hard brown bread left on the tray on the bedside table. As he broke his fast, he eyed the rumpled bedsheets.

Last night, Agata had shyly mentioned her dream of becoming a mother.

He'd joked about looking forward to making it possible, but in reality, the idea was more than a little terrifying. He'd barely begun to get his life in order once more, and it was entirely thanks to his new wife. Raising Callan was enough of a challenge, and the boy was already half grown.

A bairn? He had to admit, as terrifying as the prospect was, the idea of watching Agata's body change while carrying their bairn… it did something odd to his heart.

If they continued the way they had last night, it might very well happen. In fact, he'd woken her sometime after midnight by fondling those glorious breasts of hers, and with her arse pressed against him like that, it'd been a simple matter of sliding inside…

Beneath the coverlet, he felt himself stir, and grinned again. It seemed his cock couldn't get enough of his wife.

Where *was* she? Had she crawled back to her own bed? Jaimie's grin faded. Did she not like sleeping with him? Well, there was a reason the lady of the keep had her own chamber. Although he had no plans on moving into the laird's chambers, mayhap he could discuss with his wife how often he could visit her room.

The thought of merely *visiting* his wife, after having her in his arms all night, was enough to sour his mood. He tossed the bread back to the trencher and swung his legs out of bed.

Her gown was gone. Had she pulled it back on before she'd left or slipped back into her room to get dressed? Her dress had been filthy, although come to think of it, she'd never answered his question of what she'd been doing to get so dirty.

His gaze rested on the tub, and his lips twitched in pleasure once more. Aye, he'd asked her that right before he'd pulled her into the bath with him, and her body had been enough of a distraction he hadn't minded her not answering him, had he?

Whatever she was doing, if she was getting dirty again, he'd take her to the loch this time. He'd strip her down right there on the shore and carry her into the water, and to hell with anyone who happened to be watching. She was his, and as far as he was concerned, he was hers.

Reaching for his kilt, he considered what had passed between them last night. When she commanded him, he was helpless to resist, but he understood what she'd been trying to teach him. He tied his hair back with the same thong she'd left him last night, made short work of dressing, then stared down at his ruined hands.

Only now, thanks to Agata, he didn't see them as quite so ruined. Aye, the fingers were stunted, and they'd never be whole again. But she'd shown him everything they *could* do. He could wield a sword and best a warrior. He could paint and hold a stylus. And he could love a woman.

Love? Aye, he was in love with Agata. And not the way he'd loved Aileen, but with something purer.

While Aileen had enjoyed influence over men—Jaimie in particular—he knew Agata had only taken control of his life because he'd been unable to. Everything she'd done for him in the last weeks had been for him, to make his life better. She was caring and capable and strong, and for some reason, she saw him as worthy enough to save.

She hadn't seen him as weak, and had proven it.

Taking a deep breath, he flexed his fingers. Whatever the future held, he knew he could face it.

But for now, he needed a nice cool drink... of water.

With his chin up and his shoulders back, he stepped out of his chamber. He paused outside the door to her room and knocked. When no one answered, he pushed open the door, expecting to find her spread under her coverlet with a satisfied grin on her sleepy face.

But she wasn't there. What was more concerning was neither was the filthy gown she'd worn yesterday. He frowned thoughtfully as he pulled the door closed once more. Had one of the servants already taken it for washing?

There was no reason for him to feel uneasy, but that didn't stop him from pondering what it meant on his way to the solar. Did she have something planned today which she'd forgotten to mention last night?

"Ye're looking satisfied, lad."

He'd been so engrossed in thought, he'd missed his aunt's arrival. Startled, he quickly recovered and nodded respectfully. "Good morning, Aunt Jean. How are ye this fine morning?"

She didn't even bother to hide her grin as she looked him over. "Not nearly as pleased as ye, I think. The keep is abuzz over the news ye and yer lady wife are finally sharing a bed."

Lifting a brow in challenge, he hid his smirk. "Oh, aye? And is that important?"

Gracefully, she conceded with a nod and a smile. "What ye do with yer wife is yer own business, Jaimie. But we're pleased our laird and lady have a strong marriage."

He was pleased, too—beyond pleased, and knew he owed much to this lady. So he lowered himself into one of the elaborate bows which used to be favored at court. "Thank ye for yer help in arranging the match, Aunt Jean."

"For forcing yer drunk arse into it, ye mean?"

Rising once more, he winked at her. "Aye, that's what I meant."

Chuckling, she reached out and tugged at his queue. "I like this, lad." Her expression softened. "It suits ye, as does this happiness. I am pleased ye found yer southern treasure!"

Uncomfortable at her praise, he cleared his throat. "Where are ye off to this morning?"

"Oh, a woman's work is never done. Agata asked me to take her place and meet with Cook about our supplies."

He nodded. "Could ye ask her to send up something to my solar?" Although the feeling of unease had returned with the mention of Agata being so busy she must share one of her duties, he knew he'd need more than a chunk of bread this morning, or he'd be grumpy all day.

"Aye, for certes, Jaimie," she said with a nod as she turned for the stairs.

"Oh, Aunt Jean? Have ye seen Agata this morning?"

He'd tried to keep his voice nonchalant, but a flicker of curiosity in her eyes when she glanced back at him told him he hadn't completely succeeded.

She slowly nodded. "I saw her and that nephew of yers when the sun was only peeking over the horizon. They were both giggling and up to something, but I didnae ask."

"Where were they?"

"In the guest hall upstairs. She was wearing that same filthy gown from yesterday, so I assumed she hadn't had time to return to her chambers, or she planned on getting dirty again. Is aught amiss?"

He shook his head and forced a grin, thanking her for the help. But as he stepped into the solar and prepared for the day's work, Jaimie was frowning.

There was no reason to be worried about his wife. So why couldn't he shake this uneasy feeling?

"WHERE IS THE SOUTH-LAND?"

Agata startled, realizing she'd been following Callan's footsteps in the dust without really seeing them. They were retracing the path they'd taken yesterday, but her heart wasn't invested in the search.

Nay, she was still abed with Jaimie.

When she'd led him into that room last night, she'd had no idea to what heights he'd take her. And how many times! She felt as if she'd barely slept a wink. When the dawn light had woken her, she remembered her promise to Callan. Slipping out of Jaimie's arms had been one of the hardest things she'd ever done, but he'd merely grunted and rolled onto his stomach as she dressed. And it was a good thing, because the lad had been waiting impatiently outside her room, candles in hand.

What had he asked her? She pinched the bridge of her nose and tried to shake away the happy exhaustion which had crept over her. "I'm sorry, lad. What did ye say?"

Luckily, he hadn't seemed to notice her distraction. He peered ahead into the darkness, carefully picking his way along the passageway with one hand on the dirty stone wall.

By the light of her candle, she saw him shrug. "I just meant, Aunt Jean is always saying something about the treasure in the south, or south-land, or something. So, I wanted to ken where that was."

Her lips twitched. "So maybe ye can go find the treasure, hmm?"

"Aye!" He took his hand away from the wall long enough to mimic a great slashing sword fight, hopping forward a few paces and making *swooshing* noises. "Every great warrior needs a quest, ye ken!"

"I ken," she said seriously, and managed not to grimace as he wiped his grimy hand on his kilt before placing it back on the wall.

A great warrior's quest? Was that what this was? If she'd been Citrine or Saffy, she might've said yes. Citrine often trained with the men and was accomplished with a sword *and* bow. She'd even dragged her twin along a few times, and they both seemed equally devoted to finding the jewels and saving their family line.

But Agata? Her great quest in life was building a stable home and having a family. Last year, or even a month ago, when she'd found that marriage contract in Da's solar, she hadn't been hopeful about her chances. But the changes Jaimie had made in the last few weeks were remarkable, and she could see herself being quite happy here with him in the future.

In the future? Nay. She smiled. If she was honest with herself, she was quite happy right now. She was certain Jaimie saw in himself what *she* saw, strength and perseverance and *worth.*

She could love a man like that.

"Aunt Agata!"

She jumped again, the candle flame flickering. "Aye?"

The little boy actually turned long enough to roll his eyes. "I *asked* where the south-land was! So I could go!"

Oh. Had she not answered that?

"'Tis just a saying, lad. Sometimes it means… well, yer father thought it to mean 'twas silly dreaming for things ye cannae have. To him, I think, it was a reminder that naught good came from looking elsewhere for fulfillment."

It was a fine summary of David Mackenzie, actually. The man was not only hard, but refused to dream, doing things the way his father before him had. Thank the good Lord that Callan was much more like his Uncle Jaimie.

Actually, after what she'd learned last night, it was possible the reason the boy was so much like Jaimie was because *he* was the lad's father. She frowned thoughtfully, no longer paying attention to the passageway or what it might lead to. What would change if Jaimie had fathered the boy? Nothing, really. Callan would still become the laird in due time, and Jaimie would lead the clan in the meantime. The two of them were growing close, sharing interests and laughter, and she couldn't ask for more.

She just wished there was a way to heal Jaimie's heart. He'd been through so much with Aileen, and Agata hated to think of how the other woman must have tried to control him. Isn't that what she was doing? Was she any better?

"I see the light!" Callan suddenly shouted, right before he darted ahead.

Sure enough, they soon came to the builder's mark on the wall and the window high above the training fields. The men were down there again, but she saw no sign of Jaimie. Was he still abed?

"This is as far as we came yesterday," Callan reminded her.

She sent him a smile. "Aye. Are ye ready to press on?"

He blew out a breath, looking very much like Jaimie for a moment while he considered. "'Twould be easier if ye told me what we were looking for."

He'd said it so seriously she had to chuckle. Reaching out to ruffle his hair, she said, "I'm sure it would be, but I told ye, I made a promise no' to reveal my quest."

His eyes brightened. "Like a blood oath?"

Well, she had no closer blood kin than her sisters, did she? "Aye, just like that!"

"I guess I cannae ask ye to break that," he said with a frown. Then, "Maybe a hint?"

"Ye ken I'm searching for information about my family, aye? So aught about the Sinclairs."

"Or a circle with other circles, ye said."

Oh, had she told him all that? She shrugged. "Aye. The clue would have to be verra old, a few generations at least. And not out in the open—'twould be hidden. That's why we're searching the secret passageways."

The lad nodded eagerly. "Can I lead again?"

He was already striding across the untouched dust, so she hurried to catch up with him. "Remember what yer uncle said! 'Tis dangerous."

Callan snorted dismissively. "I'm *always* careful."

Sure enough, he was the one who saw the missing floorboards before she did. They were in a portion of the passage where both walls were stone, but she was already so disoriented she couldn't tell what part of the keep they were near. Were there other doors or entryways they'd missed? Surely not here in the stone.

The floor was still wooden, but here the boards had rotted away, or never been installed at all. Instead, a stone ledge followed along the outer wall.

"Well, now I see what Jaimie meant," she said thoughtfully, holding the candle out over the depths. The light didn't penetrate far, and it was impossible to see how far the fall would be. "'Tis time to turn back."

"Nay!" the boy said with disappointment. "Look, 'tisnae too far!"

And before she could stop him, he'd scampered along the ledge to the other side. The scream had barely time to gather in her throat before he turned to her, arms held wide and a proud grin on his face.

"See?" he nearly crowed. "Naught to worry about!"

Her heart was still pounding at the sight of him balancing above the nothingness. "Callan Mackenzie," she finally managed to grate out, "Dinnae *ever* do something so *rash,* so *reckless—*"

"Ye wanted to find clues, aye? Pass me yer candle."

It was clear the scamp wasn't going to apologize. It was also clear that this patch wasn't nearly as dangerous as she'd thought. Sighing, she gave the lad a good frown to let him know what she thought of his recklessness.

He grinned incorrigibly.

After passing him the candle—the hole was really no more than an arms-reach—she took a deep breath and stepped onto the ledge. She was too big to fit the same as Callan, so she ended up turning sideways and bracing her hands against the opposite wall to balance herself as she shuffled across. Thank goodness the passageway was narrow!

When she made it to the other side, the boy's grin grew. "Good work, Aunt Agata."

Lord help me.

"I'll go first this time, if ye please," she said, moving in front of the seven-year-old, who bowed extravagantly as she passed.

She just barely hid her smirk.

The next moments passed in silence, with her moving much slower than Callan had, testing each new section of floor carefully before putting her weight on it. Finally, from behind, he spoke again.

"Aunt Agata? What does Aunt Jean mean when she talks about the south-lands?"

"Hmm?"

"Well, ye told me what my father meant when he said it. But when Aunt Jean uses it, she means something else, I ken it."

Agata halted while she thought about it. "I suppose for her, it's more about hoping. When she speaks of her southerly treasure, she means something good worth hoping for." David had always said that wishing was silly, but Agata knew it was important for everyone to have hope.

"Oh." The boy sounded so disappointed she turned. "Ye mean there's not really a treasure south of here?"

She ruffled his hair once more. "I dinnae ken where or how the saying started, lad, but I think the 'treasure in the south-land' is just a way of…"

Trailing off, she pursed her lips thoughtfully. Treasure in the south-land? To a Sinclair, practically *everything* was in a southerly direction. Mackenzie land certainly was. If someone asked her, she'd say *Jaimie* was her south-land treasure. Jaimie and Callan and the happiness she'd found here.

But that made no sense, because she'd never heard the phrase outside of Mackenzie land. They were in the west, so while many lands lie south of them, there were still clans to the north as well. Finally, she shrugged.

"I suppose we could always ask Aunt Jean. She might ken the origin of the phrase, since she's always using it."

"Aye!" The boy brightened. "She's *ancient!*"

While Agata pressed her knuckles to her lips to keep from laughing, the boy slipped around her in the passageway.

How would Jean react to being called ancient? Chuckling silently, Agata shook her head and turned to follow the boy. Jean was by no means elderly, but she *was* old enough to mayhap know the phrase's origin. While it probably had little relevance, it was a mystery, just like the disappearance of the Sinclair jewels.

"Aunt Agata, do ye think—"

She never found out what he'd been about to ask her, because Callan cut off his question with a sudden gasp, which was accompanied by a sound which caused her stomach to drop. They were used to the creak of the ancient floorboards, but this was more of a *cracking* noise.

Time seemed to slow as she darted forward, intent on saving the lad.

He'd just turned to her when the wood gave out from under him, and she saw his precious eyes widen with terror in the light of the candle he held.

Nay!

Grabbing his arm, she spun, intent on using her momentum to push him back the way they'd come. The floorboards had seemed sturdy there, and she prayed they'd hold.

Please God, please God, please God, she chanted silently in beat with her swiftly pounding heart as she swung Callan back toward safety.

He stumbled back toward the firm footing, his candle sputtering in the wind of their movements, as Agata's momentum carried her out over the rotten wood. Her first footfall seemed fine, but her second went *through* the floor, and by the time she stumbled on, the floor was just... gone.

She heard Callan scream her name as she twisted in midair and made a desperate grab for the edge of the floor, but it was in vain. She had just enough time to meet his terrified eyes before she fell into darkness.

CHAPTER 11

Jaimie hadn't been able to shake that uneasy feeling. More than once that morning he'd had to re-read a passage or re-calculate percentages, because his mind was too distracted. And despite what Aunt Jean had teased him about, it wasn't because he was thinking about his night with Agata. Nay, it was because of the odd *expectant* feeling in his stomach.

With a muttered curse, he tossed down the scroll he'd been reading and watched it hit the ever-present wooden map and slither off the side. It was a good thing Edward wasn't there with him this morning; nothing was getting done.

He stood and crossed to the window. Should he forget attempting to work and go find her? Would that send her the wrong message, that he couldn't manage to be parted from her? But that was the truth, he admitted with a frown. He *didn't* want to be parted from her, and just the fact that she wasn't here was making him anxious.

Or was it more than that?

He sighed and scrubbed his hand through his hair. When he pulled it from its queue, he absentmindedly pulled it back and re-tied it, still frowning. Where had she and Callan gone off to? Jean said she'd seen them in the upper story, but Agata had been dressed in the same gown from yesterday.

If she wasn't planning on being out-of-doors... Jaimie's head snapped up in realization.

The passageways.

Nay, surely they wouldn't go in there? He'd expressly told them not to go into the passageways without him, because they were so dangerous. And Agata was intelligent enough to... he groaned. He *hadn't* told them not to go into the passages. He'd told them not to go *alone*.

I'll wager they both took that to mean they could go together.

Memory flashed, hard and sharp, of a summer years ago. Father and David had told him not to go into the passages, but he'd been convinced he could handle whatever dangers lurked, and the hint of mystery was too enticing.

He'd fallen through the floor where the wood had rotted and gashed his arm so badly infection and fever set in. He'd only escaped punishment because Aunt Jean had lied to his father when asked if Jaimie had disobeyed.

"Damn."

The thought of Callan being hurt was enough to send Jaimie striding for the desk and scooping up the candle stand. It gave faint light here in the bright solar, but would be essential if he was to go into the passages.

Dear God in heaven, let me be wrong.

Still, better to check the most dangerous place first, to eliminate that possibility, before checking other parts of the castle.

The hidden entrance in the solar wasn't one he'd used as a lad, but he'd discovered it when he'd first returned to the keep after David's death. Now, he held the candle high as he pulled his dagger from his belt, wedged it into the crack, and levered the door open.

Taking a deep breath, he stepped into the darkness. He

kept his foot against the door so light filtered in, and knew from experience it wouldn't swing closed without some effort. There were footprints in the dust at his feet, but they were too muddled to be any help. Muddled… as if by a trailing gown?

Peering down the passage, first one way, then the other, he strained to catch some indication of which direction he should begin his hunt.

There! Footsteps?

Relief flooded his veins at the same moment he understood he'd been right. Callan and Agata *were* in the passages, and judging from how fast those footsteps were coming, something was wrong.

He began moving in their direction. Soon the sound of pounding footsteps was accompanied by harsh breathing, the panting of a young lad.

Jaimie's stomach climbed into his throat as he began to jog, praying he remembered the dangerous places enough to avoid them. Callan was somewhere ahead, and he was afraid.

"Callan?" he called. "Are ye hurt? I'm coming, lad!"

He heard a noise which may have been a whimper or his whispered name, but it was full of fear. The footsteps actually sped up, if possible, and within moments, he saw the lad's light as he came around a corner ahead.

"Callan!"

Oh, thank God, he looks whole.

The boy crashed into him, and they both held their candles safely away as Jaimie wrapped his free hand around the lad and buried his face in his disheveled hair.

"I was so worried," he murmured. "Why did ye come in here alone?"

Callan began to struggle in his hold, so Jaimie pulled away just enough to see the lad's face.

And realized, despite their reunion, Callan was still terrified. Dread washed over Jaimie, making his limbs go numb.

Agata.

He forced a breath and tightened his hold on Callan's shoulder. "What is it, lad?"

When the boy spoke, it was everything Jaimie had dreaded. "Agata," he gasped. "That way. She fell."

Fell? Dear God, nay!

Jaimie shoved the boy toward the exit to his solar. "Get help," he yelled, already running down the passage. "Find a servant and organize—"

He cut himself off with a curse when he realized Callan was following him.

"Nay! She said to get *ye*, Uncle Jaimie, no' some weak servant!" The boy's breaths were coming in pants now, but Jaimie understood what he'd said.

Cannae fault the boy's loyalty.

But the terror which had taken hold of his mind as soon as he'd heard Agata had fallen meant *he* was the weak one. But... but if Agata had told Callan what to do, told him who to fetch, then that meant she was still alive. If she could still speak, there was hope.

The knowledge gave his legs strength. "Then try to keep up!" he yelled to his nephew as he increased his stride, pounding along the ancient passage.

He was barely thinking at this point, but some part of his mind—or maybe just his body—remembered the spot in the floor which had given away with such disastrous consequences all those years ago. When he came to the hole, he didn't bother stopping or bracing against the stone ledge; he just gathered his momentum and leapt, landing solidly on the other side on the firm wood, all without breaking his stride.

He heard Callan shuffling along behind him across the ledge, and forced himself to slow. If the wood was weaker here, the new damage could be up ahead. But as soon as he heard Callan safely cross, he turned his attention forward once more.

"Agata?" he called, not even sure if he was expecting a response. "I'm coming!"

"Jaimie!"

Her reply was weak and distant, but he could hear her relief. He cursed again and began to run once more.

"Uncle Jaimie!" Callan had been slowing, so his voice came from farther back. "No' too far now."

The boy's warning came just in time. Jaimie skidded to a stop as the forward edge of the light he carried illuminated the broken boards where she must've fallen. Quickly, he wedged the candle stand against the wall, praying it would continue to provide the light they needed, and threw himself down on his stomach. Hopefully, by distributing his weight that way, no further floorboards would give way.

"Agata?" he called again, his heart in his throat as he inched his way closer to the hole. "Love, can ye hear me?"

"Oh, thank ye, Jaimie!"

He heard her release a breath just as he reached the edge of the rotten section, and his eyes widened at what he saw.

Agata had fallen, aye, but unlike his fall so many years ago, she hadn't been able to catch the lip of the boards. Instead, she must've thrown out her hands to either side to catch herself. Thank God the passage was so narrow, because she hung, one hand and one foot braced on either wall, above sheer nothingness.

Her arms were already trembling as she met his eyes. "Tell me ye brought a rope?"

"Nay." He quickly shifted forward until his hips held his weight, and his shoulders and head were out over the void. "But I can reach ye if ye give me yer hand," he said gently, trying to sound confident.

Her expression turned panicked, and he could tell how difficult this position was for her. "Nay! If I let go, I'll fall."

His smile was forced, but he did his best to keep her calm, holding her beautiful gaze. "Love, I swear to ye, I willnae let ye fall. 'Tis just a wee adventure. In the time it will take ye to swing one arm up toward me, I'll grab it, and be holding ye afore ye could even think about falling."

She was silent for a long moment, her eyes studying him. Finally, she took another breath. "Swear it, Jaimie?"

"I swear it, love," he answered immediately.

She shuddered and squeezed her eyes shut. "I cannae!"

His heart clenched at her wail. She was so strong, so determined. But now...? Now it was up to him to be in control.

"Agata, look at me." At his harsh command, her terrified gaze found his once more. "Ye *will* grab my hand, do ye hear me? And ye'll do it when I say so. Understand?"

Her eyes widened in surprise, and he took that as an "aye."

"On the count of three, Agata," he said, keeping his voice hard. "One, two, *three*!"

At his command, she took a deep breath and released her hold on the wall. As she lost her grip on the other three points of contact, she swung her hand up toward him, and he knew he had only one moment to get it right.

He did.

Their hands clasped, and he used the momentum of her swing to grab her other arm. Her weight pulled him forward, but he grunted and flexed his feet against the passage walls. Then, as he began to pull her upright, he felt something press against his arse and realized Callan had arrived and was helping to anchor him.

Jaimie couldn't waste any breath calling encouragement, but he concentrated on lifting Agata from the hole. She helped where she could, kicking against the wall to help push upward.

And then, with one last heave, she was up and over the lip of the floor. He rolled to one side, dislodging Callan, and pulled her into his arms. With his face buried in the crook of her neck, he breathed in her scent and thanked God for her safety.

She mumbled something against his neck, but he couldn't make himself loosen his hold on her.

"I was so scared," he admitted in a harsh whisper against her skin. "I was… I've never been so scared in my life."

She was the one who pulled away, but just far enough to peer up at him. "Never? No' even when Aileen died?"

At the mention of his mother, Callan whimpered and threw himself at Agata. She wrapped one arm around him while she looked up at Jaimie, who shook his head.

"Nay." He took a deep breath and gathered Callan in the circle of his arms as well. With his family safe, he admitted the truth. "I wasnae scared then. I accepted that my fate was what I'd deserved, because I was weak. But I wasnae scared."

Smiling, she reached up and cupped his cheek, her fingertips caressing his face. "Ye're no' weak, Jaimie Mackenzie. Ye're the strongest man I ken."

He shifted his hold and reached up to grab her hand. Turning his head, he pressed a kiss into her palm. "Only thanks to ye, Agata. I'd be naught without ye."

Miraculously, her smile grew. "Ye ken what that means, do ye no'?"

He met her eyes and nodded. "Aye," he breathed. "I love ye. I love ye more than I ever thought I'd love another person."

"Good. Because I love ye, too. Ye're a wonderful man, Jaimie, and I'm proud to be yer wife."

In her arms, Callan whimpered and burrowed his head further in her chest. She chuckled, even while Jaimie was still reeling from her confession.

"And I love ye, too, wee one," she said gently to the boy. "That was a verra brave thing ye did, getting yer uncle for me."

Jaimie cleared his throat, knowing the lad needed praise. "Aye, Callan. I'll always be in yer debt, for saving Agata." His gaze crept back to hers. "Truly, wife? Ye love me?"

Her fingers were still wrapped in his, but she managed to twist until they were intertwined. "Truly. I love ye, husband. And ye too, Callan." She dropped a kiss to the lad's head. "Ye both are my southern treasures."

The phrase made Jaimie frown in confusion. "Yer what?"

For the first time, Callan pulled away and sat up. Without his weight on them both, Agata pushed herself upright as well, as Jaimie helped. The lad was obviously eager to participate.

"Aunt Jean always talks about the treasure in the southern lands."

"Aye," Agata said, laughing as she grabbed the lad's hand in her free one. "And to a Sinclair, *every* land is a southern land! So I just meant—"

When she sucked in a sudden breath and her eyes went wide, Jaimie actually tensed, looking for the new danger. But she just stared over his shoulder, as if entranced. He actually twisted around, hoping to catch a glimpse of whatever had captured her attention, but had no luck.

"Agata?" he asked gently.

"I just…" As if in a daze, her eyes landed on his once more. "I figured it out," she whispered. "What if… what if the saying is *true?*"

Callan gave a little bounce. "Ye mean there really *is* a treasure?"

"Aye." She nodded and gave a wry laugh. "I made a promise not to tell, but while dangling helplessly and near death, I made *another* promise to myself to tell both of ye."

"Tell us! Tell us!" the boy begged.

Jaimie listened to her tell him the oddest story of missing jewels and a clan on the brink of disaster.

When she was finished, Callan sat stunned, but Jaimie shook his head. "What does this tale have to do with aught?"

"When we found the tapestry, we confronted our old nurse. She confirmed that our grandmother had given her the tapestry and entrusted its care to her. We were convinced there was a clue there, and we'd be able to find the jewels and restore our clan's glory."

"And were ye?"

Callan sighed in exasperation. "Of course, Uncle Jaimie. That's why she's *here!*"

When he raised his brow in question, Agata smiled and nodded. "We discovered this at the same time I found my marriage contract. No' only that, but the only word on the tapestry was the Mackenzie name. So I kenned that by coming here, I could fulfill my duty to my father *and* find a possible link to the missing jewels!"

Jewels. Wasn't that what she was called? The Sinclair daughters were their father's jewels. As far as he was concerned, she was far more precious than any missing brooch.

"And now?" he asked doubtfully.

"And now," she repeated in a breathless whisper, "I think I *have* found the link!"

"My aunt's saying?"

When she shook her head, her honey-blonde hair whisked around her shoulders. "No' just yer aunt, but yer brother as well. Jean told me it was something *her* grandmother used to say, aye? But I've never heard it beyond yer family. What if 'tis a *clue?*"

Callan gasped. "The same as the tapestry? Someone left ye a trail? Southern lands? Ye have to go to the Sutherlands next!"

Agata nodded, as excited as the seven-year-old. "The Sutherlands have the jewels!"

"Actually..." Jaimie hardly dared to whisper the tendril of thought which snaked through his memory at that moment. Something innocuous, something he'd seen every day... "They might *not*."

Unwilling to say more in case just by speaking the idea he made it untrue, he reached for the candle holder and stood, holding one hand out to his wife. He gently lifted her to her feet, feeling the way her muscles shuddered after their ordeal. Holding her close, he watched Callan scramble to his feet, then jerked his head to tell the boy to lead them back.

They moved deliberately, with Jaimie taking special care of Agata, in case it was too much for her. But of course, he needn't worry, she was strong. When it came time to cross the hole Jaimie had made all those years ago, she went with only a small whimper. It was hard to allow her to step out again, but Jaimie was by her side, whispering encouragements.

I love ye. I love ye.

Her words thrummed through his mind in time with his own heartbeat as the trio shuffled silently through the passageways. No one spoke, all too intent on discovering Jaimie's secret, and he prayed he wasn't wrong.

The door to his solar was still open, and Callan slipped through, then held it wider for them. Which was good, because Jaimie couldn't seem to let Agata go. With his arm around her waist and her pressed up against him, he felt... *whole*. And not the way he'd felt last night, bollocks-deep in her. Nay, this was something more. Something more *meaningful*.

I love ye. I love ye.

With a deep breath, he released her, allowing her to slide to the high-backed chair which used to be David's. She should be shivering, but she was too strong for that. Her bright eyes, with their flecks of gold, turned to him in excitement.

"Jaimie?" she prompted him.

Instead of answering, he turned to the desk and began sweeping away the scrolls and documents Edward had left for him. Taking a deep breath, he grabbed ahold of the ancient carved map and dragged it closer to his family.

"Oh!" Callan exclaimed, bouncing in excitement. "I ken this!" He spoke to Agata as one finger stabbed at the various delineations. "Uncle Jaimie taught me the clans with this. See? This is us! And the MacLeods are up here, and this is the MacDonells and the Rosses here."

"And this," Jaimie said softly, knocking on the wooden area between the Mackenzies and the Sinclairs, "is the Sutherlands."

"The Sutherlands," Agata breathed, leaning forward to peer at what had once been a beautifully painted piece of art. "The southern lands." Her hands hovered above the wood, as if afraid to touch it. "Do ye think… it's *there*?"

"This was the map my father used to learn the clans from *his* father. Boundaries have changed, and the paint's worn off," Jaimie used his thumbnail to scrape off a blue flake, "but 'tis been in my family for generations. The same as the saying."

"Mayhap for as long as the Sinclair jewels have been missing!" Agata smiled.

And despite his efforts not to get his hopes up, Jaimie found himself smiling in return. "There's only one way to find out."

Callan bounced again. "Do it! Do it!"

Jaimie slid his dagger from his belt and handed it, hilt first, to Agata. "Ye do the honors, love. I ken what I can do with these fingers now… and what I cannae do."

When he winked at her, she blushed, and it made his heart soar.

Taking the dagger, she leaned over the map, her delicate touch tracing the deeply inscribed borders of each clan. "I think…" She licked her lips and peered closer, intent on the mystery. "I think ye're right, Jaimie."

With a deep breath, she carefully pressed the tip of the dagger into one of the indentions, and—miracle of miracles—*wiggled* it!

All three of them sucked in gasps as she pressed gently on the dagger's hilt. With a creak of wood, the Sutherland borders gave way, and a piece of the map *popped off.*

He could see her hands shaking as she reached into the hole left in the map. It wasn't very deep. Nay, it was just deep enough and just wide enough—thanks to the Sutherland's wide territory—to contain a linen-wrapped *something*. He watched her place it over the Lowlands and began slowly unpeeling the wrapping.

Both he and Callan were leaning over the mysterious package when she, at last, revealed the contents, and both of them reared back in disbelief. For her part, Agata's whispered, "Aye!" told him she'd never doubted.

Sitting there in the midst of creamy linen was the largest, roundest agate he'd ever seen. Easily three or four times the size of a man's thumbnail, it was the exact same sable-and-gold shade as his wife's eyes. It must've taken a master craftsman many days to fashion such a perfect circle from an unblemished stone.

With shaking hands, Agata slowly picked up the jewel and closed her fingers around it, as much as she was able to. Her breathing was slow and steady as she turned wonder-filled eyes up at Jaimie.

"Ye found it, husband," she whispered. "My jewel!"

The laughter burst out of him with his breath, and he reached down to pull her into his arms. "That rock can be *yer* jewel, wife, but I've found *my* jewel right here."

She was laughing with him, although he didn't know if it was in relief or joy. "I love ye, Jaimie Mackenzie!"

"And I love ye, my strong wife. Thank ye for making me the man I am."

She cupped his cheek, sobering slightly. "I didnae, husband. Ye've been that man all along. I just reminded ye he was there."

God, how he loved this woman. Staring down at her, he knew he might struggle, knew he might fall… but with her by his side, he'd always be improving. "I love ye," he whispered again. "Ye've made my life perfect."

When his lips claimed hers, Callan made gagging noises in the background, and that was perfect, too.

EPILOGUE

THE SUMMER SUN shown gaily through the window in her husband's solar, but Agata had still lit the candles to better illuminate her work. She was bent over the desk, the pot of glue mixed with white paint by her elbow, and she hummed as she applied the next layer of base to the ancient map. With Jaimie's permission, she'd sanded the remains of the paint off, and was preparing the family heirloom to be repainted.

By her.

The knowledge this map would be used by future generations made her throat tighten with emotion. Painting was so important to her, and once she'd been able to share it with Jaimie and Callan, her two loves, she didn't think she'd be more satisfied. But by performing this restoration, her work would be seen for many, many years.

It was humbling and exciting, all at once.

"Should ye be doing that, in yer condition?"

Agata jumped at Aunt Jean's sharp words, but managed to keep from ruining the smooth line of glue her wide brush was applying. Holding her breath, she finished the stroke and returned the brush calmly to the pot, before fixing the old woman with a glare.

"Are ye no' supposed to knock?"

Jean waved away the chastisement before sinking into Edward's chair. "Only when I ken yer husband is in here with ye. That's a mistake I'll no' make again, let me tell ye."

Agata's cheeks burned at the reminder of being caught sitting on Jaimie's lap last week, but she lifted her chin and tried for a stern tone. "And what do ye mean, *my condition?*"

"The babe, lass!" Jean's eyes twinkled with teasing.

"I'm no' pregnant, Aunt Jean."

The old woman waggled her brows. "Yet, eh?"

This time Agata couldn't hold her gaze, and *did* look down at the map with a flush. *Yet.* In the few weeks since Jaimie had declared his love for her, she was still easing into their new lives. And as much as she wanted to be a mother, she knew these things took time.

"Mayhap," she whispered.

The way she and Jaimie were with one another, they might be well on their way to making a bairn sooner rather than later, God willing. Or mayhap she was unable to carry a babe, which would explain why David's seed didn't take. If that was the case, Agata knew her love for Callan, and his for her and Jaimie, would fill her heart just fine.

Jean, bless her, changed the subject. "Any word from yer sisters?"

Agata couldn't help but grin as she met the old woman's eyes again. "Aye! I told them of everything we found here, when Jaimie sent the courier and guards with the jewel we found."

In the aftermath of their discovery, Agata and Jaimie had explained everything to Jean, although they'd asked her not to tell Edward or the others. The old woman had been helpful.

"And ye told them what I kenned of the saying? How I

recall my grandmother using it, and how I always thought it was just a clever phrase?"

"Aye, but it's more interesting that yer grandmother was a Campbell, because Saffy read through our histories, and our great-grandfather's second wife was a Campbell as well!"

Jean's eyes shown with matching excitement. "Does she—do ye think there's a relation?"

"We dinnae ken yet, but it's intriguing. What if our ancestress—only, she's no' really, since she was our great-granda's second wife—sent yer grandmother here with the jewel, and the phrase has been passed down as a hint?"

Jean blew out a breath and sat back in her chair, shaking her head in amazement. "'Tis impossible to ken now, I suppose. But whether it was meant or no', the phrase certainly led ye to the jewel. Were yer sisters pleased to have it returned?"

Agata nodded. "Aye, although they're still arguing over what to do with it. Saffy wants to share it with the clan, to prove the legend is wrong and our line isnae cursed. Citrine is determined to find *all* the jewels and return them together."

Jean chuckled as she shook her head again. "One day I'd like to meet this sister of yers. What's her next step?"

"They agree the fact the agate was found under the Sutherland map is suspicious, especially since Pearl was initially supposed to marry the Sutherland laird. Saffy writes that she and Citrine agree that someone needs to investigate the Sutherlands, but I cannae imagine she means *her*." Agata chuckled at the outlandish idea. "Going to the Sutherlands would require daring, now the marriage contract has been broken, and Saffy is no' nearly as bold as Citrine."

Mayhap a man would have argued the Sinclair Jewels go to their father with the information and request his help. But not Jean. She just smiled and nodded encouragingly. "I shall pray for their success. It would be wonderful if they were to find the rest of the jewels in the Sutherland holding."

"Aye," Agata agreed. "Or even *one*. I dinnae believe in the magical ability of the brooch to suddenly bring prosperity to our clan. But if our people could see the return of our jewels, mayhap they'd stop believing our line is doomed and work with Da to find a solution. The legend says only the bravest and worthiest Sinclair can restore the jewels, but *also* that warrior will lead the clan to glory."

"And mayhap that warrior will be the next laird?"

Agata shrugged, reaching for her brush once more. "I think 'tis what Saffy hopes, but Citrine is irritated by the notion."

She and Jean discussed more theories as Agata finished the layer and cleaned her brush. The glue and white paint would dry and be sanded down to form a surface as smooth as canvas. The carved lines would probably need to be re-inscribed before she could paint them black, and the labor of love would occupy her well into the winter.

As would her new family.

Footsteps in the hall told her she'd conjured her loves with her thoughts. Jaimie stepped through the door, looking more handsome than ever. Although he hadn't cut his long black hair, he wore it pulled back at the base of his neck, and she loved being able to look into his eyes... as well as the fact he'd gained the confidence to allow his people to see his true self.

The weeks since he'd fought the drink seemed a distant memory now, with how his shoulders had broadened, and she knew for a fact he was strong. He walked now, a serious frown on his face, his hands clasped behind his back, nodding thoughtfully to whatever Callan was chattering on about.

The boy walked beside his uncle, his tiny kilt askew, his hands clasped behind his back, his dark hair tucked behind his ears. The fact he was mimicking his hero made Agata's heart swell with happiness.

She hurried to push aside her supplies and reached for the pitcher of cold water she always had waiting for Jaimie. Although the cravings had lessened the longer he went without spirits, she knew he still appreciated not having to ask for a drink. She was always there with water when the urge came upon him.

Jaimie's gaze came up and rested on her. He saw the cup of water in her hand and smiled softly. Sweet Mother Mary, he was handsome. She remembered the first time she'd seen him, on their wedding day in the chapel. She'd thought him hideous then, but it hadn't been because of his scars. Nay, it'd been because of the pain and anger she'd seen in him.

They might not ever know the truth about Callan's parentage. They might not ever know the truth of the jewels. They might never know the truth of Aileen's motives when she'd manipulated his heart.

But Agata would go to her grave knowing Jaimie loved her as much as she loved him.

And that was truly a miracle.

He crossed to the desk, took a long draught of the water, and wrapped his arm around her waist. "Have ye finished yer work, wife?"

Her brows rose. "Aye. Once this layer dries, I can—"

"Good." He plunked the cup down on the desk, wrapped his other arm around her, and lowered his lips to hers.

Agata *might have* protested that Jean and Callan were standing *right there*, except suddenly, she didn't seem to care.

It was a long moment before Callan's laughter penetrated, and Agata pulled away from Jaimie with a gasp. It didn't seem to stop her husband though, as he just switched his attention to her neck. She intended to remind him his chamber—which she now shared—wasn't far away, but his lips were sending the most wonderful sensations down to her belly and *lower*.

Dimly, she heard Jean chuckle and say, "Come, lad, let's leave them to their *work*, aye?" and then the door closed.

"Jaimie!" she gasped. "What are ye doing?"

He'd managed to pull the neckline of her gown low enough to plant kisses on the upper slopes of her breasts, but he pulled away and smiled up at her wryly.

"What does it *feel* like I'm doing, wife?"

Feel. She loved that he could feel again. She buried her fingers in his hair. "I ken what it feels like, but I wonder *why* ye would attack yer wife in the middle of the day like this."

"Attack?" he replied, as if affronted. "I'm merely showing my wife how much I adore her."

She liked the sound of that. "And how much is that, *hmm*?"

He met her challenge with a grin. Pulling one hand from his hair, he guided it to the front of his kilt. She sucked in a breath when she felt his hard length straining against the wool. When she gripped it, his pleased groan sent a surge of dampness between her thighs.

"Verra much indeed," he murmured, already reaching for the hem of her gown. "I adore ye, Agata."

AUTHOR'S NOTE

The art techniques described in this book are as accurate as I can make them.

I am indebted to Carl Garris of Columbia University, who sat patiently and let me pick his brain about medieval painting techniques while he told me all about his experiences reproducing colors. It was a serendipitous meeting which allowed me to deepen Agata's commitment to her art.

I hope you're ready to discover more details behind the mystery of the missing Sinclair brooch! Now that one jewels has been found, is there hope for the other three? Does the next clue rest with the Sutherlands?

The Sutherland Devil is feared throughout the Highlands... surely scholarly Saffy isn't going to be the one to volunteer to search his home? How will she manage?

Get ready for one of my all-time favorite books, as we see the "chicks in pants" trope come to life! Saffy is going to risk it all when she accidentally becomes the Devil's own squire in *The Sutherland Devil*! Keep reading for a sneak peek!

Before we get to Saffy and Merrick, I want to offer you a personal invitation to join my reader group – Caroline's Cohort. If you're on Facebook, I hope you'll consider becoming a part of my group. It's where I post all the best book news first, and you'll be able to get to know me personally. My Cohort group is also instrumental in helping me name characters and choose covers, so stop on by!

SNEAK PEEK

From *The Sutherland Devil!*

The Sinclair laird was ailing, and his daughters could tell, despite his blustery attempts to hide it. He sat in the large chair in his solar, the same as always, but his face was pale, and his hands gripped the wooden arms, as if to keep them from shaking.

"Ye'll be married to the MacLeod lad, and that's the end of it! I'll hear no more arguing," he growled, glaring at the twins in front of him.

Unconsciously, Saffy plucked at the threads of her kirtle, glancing at her sister. Of the two of them, the middle of the Sinclair sisters, Citrine was far braver. Or mayhap, just more foolhardy. She stood now, her hands on her hips, her foot tapping as she frowned fiercely at her father.

"Nay, Da, I'll no' marry some *boy* when ye clearly need me here!"

Saffy did her best to hide her wince, knowing Dougal, the Sinclair commander, was watching stoically. Her twin never backed down from a confrontation, but Da clearly wasn't up to arguing. Besides, it's not as if they hadn't known this was coming. Da had already married off his oldest and youngest daughters. The twins were the only ones left.

Their father labored to pull himself forward, the glare he was sending Citrine reminding Saffy very much of his old self. "I do *no'* need ye here, girl! I'm yer laird and father, and if I say ye're to marry for the betterment of the clan, then ye'll do so!"

Citrine stomped her foot. Actually stomped her foot like a child, which just showed how much she'd lost control. "Da! Ye're ill! Ye cannae ask me—"

"'Tis naught," the older man said, looking exhausted as he sank back in his chair. "I'll be better in nae time." He cocked his head slightly, studying the two of them. "But ye're good daughters to worry so. I'll no' send ye away yet."

Behind him, Dougal made a noise of disapproval. Saffy's eyes flicked to the large man, who glared at the two of them with his arms folded across his chest. He was Da's right-hand man, and always had the Sinclairs' best interest in mind. But she couldn't remember him ever staring at her or one of her sisters with such disgust before.

Da might believe this illness was naught, but he lacked the strength to even glare at his commander. "Ye think I made the wrong decision, Dougal?" he asked mildly.

"Aye," came the growled response. "Ye coddle them. Citrine's duty is to strengthen the alliance with the MacLeods, and I'll be happy to be the one to drag her to her wedding, if ye cannae."

Saffy actually backed up a step at the threat in the man's voice. Since Da had started on this mission to see his daughters married, Dougal had been an enthusiastic supporter. Did he really care so much he'd *force* Citrine to go?

But where Saffy was cautious, Citrine was daring. She strode *toward* the desk. "Ye think ye could *drag me* somewhere?"

Dougal lowered his arms. "There's naught ye could do to stop me, lass."

Citrine was a fair hand with a sword and bow, but Dougal had been the one to teach her what she knew, and he was probably right. Saffy was already moving to pull her twin back when Da spoke.

"Enough." He winced as he rubbed his stomach, and all three of them turned to him in concern. The old man waved away their stares and pulled himself upright once more. "Citrine *will* marry, but when I say. She is a loyal Sinclair, a good daughter, and a proud Jewel. Aye?"

Citrine's shoulders heaved as she tried to calm her breathing, and the muscles in her jaw twitched. Saffy reached out to take her twin's hand, offering what support she could.

"Aye, Da," Citrine finally ground out. "I'll follow yer orders." Her glare moved to Dougal. "But no' yet."

When she turned to stalk out of the room, Saffy kept a tight hold on her hand, leaving herself no opportunity to curtsey or take her leave. But it didn't seem to matter, the door slammed shut behind them, and Citrine continued her angry walk until they reached their own chamber.

"Can ye believe that man?"

Saffy released her sister while she sank down on the big bed. She and Citrine used to share it with Agata and Pearl, until they'd been married only a short time ago.

"We expected this, Citrine," she said softly, part calming, part regretful.

Da hadn't mentioned anything about a marriage contract for *her*. While she wasn't sure if she really did want to go off to be some man's wife, the *not knowing* was worse. During the winter, Da had announced he'd be looking for marriage alliances for his four daughters, the Sinclair Jewels. Agata, the eldest, had already been married and widowed by then, but Da announced Pearl's contract first, to the Sutherland Devil.

The man was twice wee Pearl's age, and rumored to be cold-hearted and vicious, caring naught for the bastards he'd spawned from here to Edinburgh. It was no surprise Pearl—who, as the youngest of the Jewels, had the closest connection to the Sinclair clan—had refused the marriage contract and instead demanded to be allowed to take holy vows. Da had reluctantly agreed, and despite Dougal's insistence on escorting Pearl—the way he'd demanded to *escort* Citrine today—had assigned his most loyal bodyguard to the task.

Saffy nor her sisters knew exactly what happened on that adventure, but Pearl and the Sinclair Hound had returned very much in love, and were now married. In fact, judging from the number of times the two of them had slipped away to the loch, she could very well be carrying Da's first grandchild.

Then, even before Pearl had returned, Agata found her marriage contract with the Mackenzies. It had been a shock, since her intended was the brother of her first husband. But her most recent letter was glowing and full of love…and news about the sisters' quest.

Aye, Citrine was the one who was most devoted to finding out what had happened to the missing Sinclair jewels—the clan brooch which was said to grant power to the laird—but Agata had done her part. And as the scholar among them, Saffy was just as excited about the possibility of solving the ancient riddle as the news her twin would be married before her.

Although, it must be nice to be wanted.

Over by the window, Citrine had halted her angry pacing and stood with her fingers laced behind her head, staring out at the summer landscape. If Saffy was known as the scholar, and Agata the lady, and Pearl the helper…then Citrine was the firebrand.

And if she wasn't burning right now, then this was a smolder.

"Citrine?" Saffy prompted carefully, not sure if she wanted to know what her twin was thinking.

"I've bought us some time," Citrine said without turning, her tone speculative. "Da willnae send me away too soon, and I'll continue to fight against Dougal's attempts to send me away. But that means I *cannae* leave."

Saffy frowned. "Wait, ye *want* to go to MacLeod land?"

Citrine scoffed without turning. "I've no desire to marry the second or fourth or ninth son of a laird. My husband will be strong!"

"Aye, but strength is no' power."

"Spoken like someone who prefers scrolls to blades," Citrine quipped, turning just enough to smirk over her shoulder.

"Spoken like someone who cannae manage to get through an entire lesson without dropping her sword."

Chuckling at the reminder of Saffy's ineptness at sparring, Citrine lowered her hands to her hips. "Ye do well enough."

"No' nearly as well as *ye*." Her twin's prowess with a blade was well-known among the clan, and she often trained with the warriors, despite Dougal's irritation. Da never seemed interested in denying this particular fire-eyed Jewel anything. But the twins' differences weren't the point. "But ye said ye were no' able to leave at all? Do ye want to leave, then?"

"No' with him so sick!" Citrine threw herself down on the bench, sprawling in a way guaranteed to make Agata scold, were she there. "Da says it's naught, but he's no' one to sicken easily. And he's no' coughing or sneezing or fevered…it's his stomach."

Saffy nodded, having noticed the same thing. "But no one else is ill."

"Aye, so we cannae even blame tainted meat…"

Citrine's musings were distracting, and Saffy shook her

head as she steered her twin back on the right course. "So ye *willnae* be leaving?"

"One of us has to."

When Saffy met her sister's golden eyes, she understood. "The jewels."

"Aye," Citrine breathed.

After Pearl's departure, the remaining sisters had found a clue to the missing brooch: an ancient tapestry from their grandmother, given to their old nurse for safe-keeping. The tapestry had pointed them to Mackenzie land, where Agata was due to journey. She spent the first weeks of her marriage searching for another clue to the missing brooch, but ultimately found one of the jewels itself.

Saffy scrambled across the bed and reached beneath to pull out the small chest where they'd stored it. Her notes and scrolls were on the top, and beneath them was the carefully folded tapestry. She sat cross-legged on the coverlet and laid each pile around her, eager to reach the bottom of the chest and the only Sinclair jewel they had.

The large agate—nigh as big as her palm—was perfectly round and smooth, flecked with gold, just like Agata's eyes. Their oldest sister and her new husband had followed a clue in an old family saying, and discovered the jewel hidden inside a wooden map of the Highlands...under the space representing the Sutherland holding.

"Ye think one of us needs to go to the Sutherlands, do ye no'?" Saffy was sure that's what her twin meant, but needed confirmation.

"Well, Pearl cannae go!" Citrine threw her hands up in exasperation. "She's our wee sister—it's my job to protect her."

"Nay, 'tis Gregor's job now."

Citrine rolled her eyes. "Aye, ye're right. But she's no' part of this mission. She's a wife now, and likely to be a mother soon, judging from the moon-eyed looks the Hound keeps giving her. The Sutherland clue Agata sent was a *good* one."

But scary. Saffy swallowed. "Mayhap we should wait for her to finish her work with the map? She said she'd write again if she found aught else."

"Like the rest of the jewels?" Citrine shook her head before Saffy could answer. "They're no' there. Were they, she would have found them already." She leaned forward and propped her elbows on her knees. "The tapestry led us to the Mackenzies, where one jewel was hidden. The Mackenzie clue is pointing us to the Sutherlands. Ye ken I'm right, Saffy."

Staring down at the large stone in her palm, Saffy had to admit the truth. "Aye." She took a shuddering breath. "And that's no' all."

Her twin shifted, excitement evident in her voice. "Ye found something in the histories?"

Reluctantly, Saffy nodded and looked up, meeting Citrine's gaze. "Remember, our great-grandsire's second wife was a Campbell?"

"Aye, and so was the Mackenzie's ancestress!"

"They were sisters."

Citrine whistled long and low while she considered the information. "So *that* would explain how the jewel got to the Mackenzie holding!"

Saffy bit her lip, unsure if she should volunteer the rest of what she'd found, knowing it would be the final piece they needed. The clue which would send either her or Citrine to the Sutherland holding, where the devil himself held court.

"Saf?" her twin prompted. "What are ye no' saying?"

There was no hiding it. "They had another sister. Who married a Sutherland."

Citrine exploded off the bench in an excited flurry of limbs. "*Aye!*" she yelled, bouncing energetically and swinging an imaginary sword. "*That's it!*" She was grinning when she turned back to Saffy, breathing heavy. "Ye've found it! Agata's clue, the Mackenzie saying, the sister connection…" She threw herself onto the bed, grabbing one of Saffy's hands. "Ye've proven that the Sutherlands have the jewels!"

"Or mayhap just another clue on this chase," Saffy cautioned.

Her sister scoffed. "Even if 'tis just another of the jewels, 'twould be fine! Having *two* of the Sinclair jewels back in the keep would be worth it! Da would—"

When she bit down on her words, Saffy squeezed her hand, knowing what she had meant to say.

A clan legend said that with the brooch—the symbol of their power—missing, the Sinclair name was bound to fall. Leadership of the clan *could* pass to one of the Jewels, but it was rumored that Duncan having only daughters was proof the legend was coming true. There would be no strong sons to take over when Da died…or was too ill to carry on. The sisters suspected that's why he was so intent on marrying them off, so they'd be safe, but Citrine had never accepted it.

The legend also said that only the strongest and bravest of the Sinclair warriors would be able to restore the jewels and the clan's future, and Saffy had often privately wondered if *that* was why Citrine trained so hard. Would her husband be as accepting of her strange skills as the Sinclairs were? Hopefully, it wouldn't matter, because the jewels would be found and legend irrelevant by the time Citrine married.

With even *two* of the jewels back home, the legend would be proved wrong. The clan would know their future would be strong—whatever the future *did* hold—and that might be enough. And hopefully, their father's health would improve.

"I still think we should tell Da about the agate and the tapestry."

Citrine's response was swift. "Nay! I—" She shook her head and pulled her hand from Saffy's grip. "I dinnae ken how to say it. This illness of his is too convenient, too coincidental. I want…" She shrugged as she pulled herself into a cross-legged position, mirroring Saffy's. "I want to be *sure* afore we present him with what we've found."

"Ye think…what? That he's been cursed?" Saffy scoffed.

Citrine shrugged. "That, or poisoned."

Gasping, Saffy shook her head. "Dinnae even *hint* at that! Who would do such a thing?"

Her twin frowned, a determined look coming to her eyes. "I dinnae ken, but I'm going to find out."

Citrine couldn't leave the Sinclair holding, not yet at least. If she left now, Da would see no reason not to send her—and Dougal—to the MacLeods for her own unwanted wedding. And if she did, that would mean she'd be unable to keep a watch on Da's illness.

And if she couldn't leave, the clue to the Sutherlands would go unstudied.

All signs pointed to the Sutherlands having a jewel, or at least there being another clue at their holding. Relations between the Sinclairs and Sutherlands had been frosty since Da had been forced to call off the wedding between Pearl and the Devil who led the other clan, so they'd be unable to approach this problem diplomatically.

One of them would have to go there, to find a way to search the keep without giving away their mission. A disguise, mayhap, to ensure the Sutherland never discovered his once-fiancée's sister under his roof?

And Citrine couldn't do it, which left…

Saffy groaned and threw herself backward on the bed, hoping she wasn't making the biggest mistake of her life.

"I'll do it."

Uh-oh! What kind of trouble could scholarly Saffy get into at the Sutherland holding? And what does she mean about a *disguise*? Get ready for one of my all-time favorite adventures (I love the way these two clash—and kiss!)...*The Sutherland Devil!*

ABOUT THE AUTHOR

USA Today bestselling author Caroline Lee has been reading romance for so long that her fourth-grade teacher used to make her cover her books with paper jackets, but it wasn't until she (mostly) grew up that she realized she could WRITE it too. So she did.

Caroline is living her own little Happily Ever After in NC with her husband, sons, daughter Princess Wiggles. She thinks it's important to note that she made it all the way through grad school (her second history degree) without knowing how to touch-type (she taught herself to type only a few years ago and APPARENTLY lesrned imcorrectly--*learned incorrectly,* a fact which she's only now realizing, as other authors point and laugh). Caroline adores rodents, goes through laptops like Pez, and never met a whisk(e)y she didn't like. She's also pretty funny in person. Promise.

You can find her at www.CarolineLeeRomance.com.

OTHER BOOKS BY CAROLINE LEE

Want the scoop on new books? Join Caroline's Cohort, an exclusive reader group! Or sign up for my mailing list by texting "Caroline" to 42828 to get started!

Hilarious Scottish RomComs:
The Hots for Scots (8 books)
Highlander Ever After (3 books)
Bad in Plaid (6 books)
Second-Chance Manor (2 books)
Those Kilted Bastards (4 books)
Surprise! Dukes (5 books)

Steamy Scottish Historicals:
The Sinclair Jewels (4 books)
The Highland Angels (5 books)

Sensual Historical Westerns:
Black Aces (3 books)
Sunset Valley (3 books)
Everland Ever After (10 books)

The Sweet Cheyenne Quartet (6 books)

Sweet Contemporary Westerns
   Quinn Valley Ranch (5 books)
   River's End Ranch (14 books)
   The Cowboys of Cauldron Valley (7 books)
   The Calendar Girls' Ranch (6 books)

Click **here** to find a complete list of Caroline's books.

*Sign up for Caroline's Newsletter to receive exclusive content and freebies, as well as first dibs on her books! Or if newsletters aren't your thing, follow her on **Bookbub** for a quick, concise new release alert every time she publishes a book!*